Also by Ce

Novels

A Thyme for Love
ThymeTable Mill
Mattie's Girl: An Appalachian Childhood
Sarranda
Journey to Stenness
Sarranda's Heart: A Love Story of Place
Sarranda's Legacy
The Body at Wrapp's Mill
The Body at StarShine Mill
The Skeleton at the Old Painted Mill

Short Stories

On a Slant: A Collection of Stories
Islands One and All: Stories and Otherwise

Anthologies Co-Edited with Nancy Dillingham

Christmas Presence: From 45 Western North Carolina Women
Writers
Clothes Lines: From 75 Western North Carolina Women
Writers
Women's Spaces Women's Places: From 50 Western North
Carolina Women Writers
It's All Relative: Tales from the Tree: From 50 WNC Women
Writers

College Textbook Co-Authored with Sally Lordeon

Writing Technical Reports: Basics and Beyond
(Canadian version) *Some Assembly Require*

Books for your Kindle:

The Body at Wrapp's Mill Kindle Edition
http://www.amazon.com/dp/B00OSMWIAQ

The Body at StarShine Mill Kindle Edition
https://www.amazon.com/dp/B01MA5IYZB

Islands One and All Kindle Edition
http://www.amazon.com/dp/B007BFRHEE

On a Slant Kindle Edition
http://www.amazon.com/dp/B00T57O7U8

Journey to Stenness Kindle Edition
http://www.amazon.com/dp/B00P5DVKFG

Sarranda's Heart: A Love Story of Place Kindle Edition
http://www.amazon.com/dp/B00CO872M0

Mattie's Girl: An Appalachian Childhood Kindle Edition
http://www.amazon.com/dp/B00QEIAM8W

Thyme Table Mill Kindle Edition
http://www.amazon.com/dp/B00PYBJNV2

Sarranda Kindle Edition
http://www.amazon.com/dp/B00PYBJ2O0

A Thyme For Love Kindle Edition
http://www.amazon.com/dp/B00U567UD4

Sarranda's Legacy Kindle Edition
https://www.amazon.com/dp/B07FPWC7PL/

Mattie's Girl

An Appalachian Childhood

Mattie's Girl

An Appalachian Childhood

Celia H. Miles

Stone Ivy Press

Published by:
Stone Ivy Press
104 Clubwood Court
Asheville, NC 28803
www.celiamiles.com

In conjunction with:
Old Mountain Press, Inc.
85 John Allman Ln.
Sylva, NC 28779
www.oldmp.com

Author photo by Mary McClurkin

Mattie's Girl: An Appalachian Childhood.

Second Edition
Printed and bound in the United States of America by Gasch Printing •
www.gaschprinting.com • 301.362.0700
10 9 8 7 6 5 4 3 2

For Louis

Acknowledgments

IF IT TAKES a village to parent a child, it takes much critiquing, encouragement, suggestions, and support from a village of fellow writers, friends, and family members to get a book to the publishable stage. I thank you all:

Yvonne Lehman and Bill Brooks, author and instructor, in whose classes the first pages were written.

The Asheville Plotters, long-time critiquers: John Alford, Mona Booth, Marshall Frank, Joan Medlicott, Kay Parkin, Bob Reynolds—all of whom have books in or awaiting publication The French Broad Writers.

And Tommy Hays, Peggy Parris and her "Finishing Your Novel" class, Ellen Price, Peggy Ryan, Joyce Parris, Frances Payne, Nancy Dillingham, Mary McClurkin, and others who saw the manuscript along the way.

About the Author

CELIA H. MILES, a native of Jackson County in western North Carolina, now lives in Asheville. She attended Brevard College and Berea College and has graduate degrees from UNC-Chapel Hill and Indiana University of Pennsylvania (IUP). She taught at Brevard College and Asheville-Buncombe Technical Community College. A long-time instructor of English, she now spends her time writing, photographing old mills and stone circles, and traveling. She has co-authored a college textbook, has published romance novels, historical and contemporary novels, along with stories and poems in various markets, and co-edited four women's writing anthologies.

Some of this material has been published in modified form in the following:

"The Big Sycamore" in *Cricket* (October 2000)
"Selling the Grit" in *Yesterday's Magazette* (July-October 1998)
"Backsliding" in *Victoria Press* (2000)
"Going to the Dentist" in *Victoria Press* (1999)

ALMOST MORE THAN A BODY CAN BEAR

A Fateful Day in April 1945

"HE WENT OFF hungry." That's all my Aunt Mattie said when the deputy sheriff and Preacher Duffey told her the news. Her husband, Sheriff Cade Geer, had been shot. "He left here hungry," she said again and sagged against the door frame. I stood with my mouth open. Couldn't move. Too much had happened this spring.

"It was them no good Rednells," Deputy Sheriff Alvin Jones said. "Fighting again. Old man beating up on them. They're not worth the paper it'd take to—" Here he stopped. The deputy was known in Jackson County for starting a string of words and not being able to finish them.

"Careful, son," the preacher said. "You didn't see what happened." He was helping Aunt Mattie to the single bed that stood to the side of the front room. "Don't say nothing that'll not hold water in court."

"Any fool knows who done it," the deputy insisted, his face red. "Don't matter if old man Rednell admits it or not."

Old man Rednell was the father of my best friend at school, PeeDee Rednell. My absolute best friend. I went to get a cloth and dipped it in the cold water bucket to spread on Aunt Mattie's forehead. I sat beside her, trying to be light on the bed. Mute. I wasn't thinking of my uncle Cade.

"Shot? At the Rednells?" I asked, wanting to be sure.

The men nodded. Aunt Mattie curled up tight as a rhododendron leaf in freezing weather. If the news itself had

1

not already made an impact on me, the sight of Mattie Geer lying on the bed with her clunky black shoes on would have. Nobody in her house put their feet on the bed with their shoes still on. I pulled a quilt over her. It didn't seem decent to have those men standing by, just watching her, waiting for a signal or something.

I glanced at the fire, low in the hearth. Deputy Jones looked, too. He turned and went out of the house toward the woodpile. This had been a cold April. I guess he was relieved to have something to do.

Preacher Duffey was holding his old felt hat in his hands, quiet. I looked at his big hands. They were clean but rough. All week he handled rocks, the best stone mason in the county, and then his two-pound black bible on Sundays.

"I've sent for Ruth and Addie to come over and stay with you tonight," he said to my aunt's back. "This child here ought to get on home."

He didn't know the big event of my week, hadn't heard, I guess. Now the big event in my nine-year old life was not very important.

Aunt Mattie mumbled something and made an attempt to unfurl herself but gave it up and lapsed back. Her head sank into the feather pillow. She wasn't crying, just sort of crouched up within herself.

"I can't go home," I told the preacher.

"Sure you can. I'll take you on Flossie if you can ride behind me. Soon as the women get here." The preacher had a car, an old Model A Ford, but half the time it wasn't running, and Flossie was his more dependable transportation.

"No, I can't. I mean, I can ride on old Flossie, I guess. But I ain't got a home no more. 'Cept here."

In the few days I'd been at Aunt Mattie's, I had been rehearsing what I'd tell PeeDee when we went back to school. Truth be told, I guess I'd been wallowing in pity, creating this big beautiful cake of "poor pitiful me," and I'd iced it with thinking about how I'd tell everybody, everybody who hadn't already heard, the news. Now my tongue didn't want to work. The preacher looked at me, his mouth slightly open.

"Mama and Daddy left me here. They're gone. I have to stay with Aunt Mattie. They may never come back."

Until I said those last words I'd practiced them in my mind. I hadn't believed them. Now I did. They wouldn't ever come back. When they had dropped me and my pillowcase full of clothes at Cade and Mattie's house, they'd had two big worn suitcases in Mr. Keever's car. Now they were gone and my uncle was dead.

"My Lord," the preacher said. Then he remembered his profession. "I mean, may the Lord have mercy on us. Gone, you say?" He looked around the room as if to seek the truth in its swept-clean-as-a-pin corners. The room was warmer near the now-blazing fire and he moved closer to it, separating himself from us. He even forgot himself to the point of putting his hat back on. That was something else Aunt Mattie wouldn't have allowed if she had been looking. Even Uncle Cade took his hat off the minute he came through the door. There was a peg for it, at both the front and back of the house.

I didn't know how much my aunt would want me to say about Mama, her husband's half-sister Rose, leaving me with her. More likely than not, it was a disgrace that she'd have to live down. After breakfast on the day school was closed because the roof blew off, Mama had piled my things on the bed and told me to put them in the pillowcase. Daddy had looked away. Then he said, "You'll be staying with your Aunt and Uncle Geer for awhile. Be a good girl, now. Don't give her and Cade no trouble."

Mama didn't even hug me, but that wasn't unusual. She just slid into the seat of the car and fluffed her hair a little. Daddy held me close and rumpled my hair. I didn't hear exactly what he said, something like "for your own good, honey." He sounded kind of choked-up when he said, "I thank ye, Mattie." I'd stayed a few times with Aunt Mattie. It didn't dawn on me right away that they were leaving me for more than a few days. Maybe forever.

And now Uncle Cade was shot over at the Rednells.

It was too much to take in. Everybody leaving.

"I'm staying here. Leastways temporarily." I might as well not reveal all my heart knew although I had said it once already. And I was mighty proud of getting to use a big word without stumbling over it.

"Temporarily?" Preacher Duffey let the word just roll off his tongue. I did admire the way he could talk.

"Where is my uncle?" Then it hit me what they hadn't actually said. "Is he dead?"

"We sent for old Doc Garret, and some of the boys'll help him bring...Yes. He's dead." The preacher's voice dropped a notch or two, but Aunt Mattie must have heard. 'Course, she surely thought the worst even if they hadn't come right out and said it. She moaned a little.

"They'll likely bring him straight here, Mattie," the preacher went on, still speaking softly and looking worried. "The women will be along directly. And I'll be back. Edith'll be wondering where I am, now it's long past dark."

Deputy Jones threw a couple of logs on the fire. Brushed his hands on his pants.

"Coldest April in a long time and the temperature's dropping. Colder than a witch's..." Naturally he didn't finish that one either.

"You stay here, Alvin," Preacher Duffey said. "I'll be going along home. The doc should be along pretty soon. Guess there's a bunch of paperwork to do. Cade being the sheriff and all."

Alvin Jones didn't look too happy about the preacher's orders, but he was young and hadn't been working more than two or three years. He was low man on the totem pole, and he wouldn't argue with Preacher Duffey, especially at a time like this. He nodded and said, "I'll get my horse under the shed. He'll be warmer than some of us, looks like."

I didn't know why he was complaining. The fire was roaring now, spreading a circle of light in the gloom. I took down the kerosene lamp from the mantle and put it on the table. The wick needed trimming but I didn't bother. I pried a sliver of pine from one of the pieces of wood on the hearth and stuck it in the fire and lighted the lamp. I hoped the deputy would stay outdoors and keep his horse company.

The preacher bent over Aunt Mattie, saying some words meant to comfort. I'd heard them before: "...in this hour of need...the Lord will sustain you...the Lord won't give you more than you can bear." He straightened up and looked at me. I rubbed my hands together and shivered.

"You stay here," he said. He must have thought I was a deputy or something, or he'd forgotten already that I was stuck here. He shook his head as if he didn't know what else he could do. I nodded and held the door open for him. Just as the clock on the mantle clanged eight times, he and Flossie disappeared out of sight down the dark road.

UNCLE CADE HAD been summoned around three hours earlier. Aunt Mattie put supper on the table at five o'clock or as close as his schedule allowed. The food had not been quite ready when he left. The cornbread was still a puffy yellow in the oven although everything sat warming on the back of the stove. Aunt Mattie had not been in a particular hurry since Uncle Cade was home, working at something in the tool shed, piddling around, she called it. My being there hadn't disrupted her day very much. Around five o'clock, one of the Rednell boys came running into the yard, panting. It was Benjy, PeeDee's younger brother. He was about eight years old, but big for his age.

"Tell your uncle to come quick," he said to me. He bent forward, hands on his knees, putting his head down, to catch his breath. The Rednells lived about three or four miles from the Aunt Mattie and Uncle Cade, going by the road. Benjy probably took some shortcuts through a pasture or two, but it was hilly and wouldn't have been an easy run.

"Yeah, what is it?" Uncle Cade came out of the shed. "More trouble at your house?"

"Mama says to come quick. Daddy's drunk, going after Marvin with a knife. Ain't caught him yet."

Uncle Cade took the porch steps two at a time and came back with his hat jammed on his head and his pistol tucked in his belt.

"Marvin keeps circling around the yard," Benjy continued. "He's afraid if he takes off, Daddy'll jump on somebody else. Daddy's crazy mad."

"Cade, you ain't had your supper yet," Aunt Mattie yelled from inside the house.

"Come on, Benjy. Let's go." My uncle hurried toward his car. "I'll be back directly, Mattie. Keep supper warm. I'm hungry."

DEPUTY JONES WARMED his backside at the fire and then paced to the window a couple of times. He didn't say anything. I didn't know what to say. This whole day was strange. He looked at me. "Any coffee back there?" He gestured toward the cook stove.

"I can heat it up."

"Be back in a minute or two to get it," he said. He went outside. I guessed he'd rather face the cold than face the silence in the room.

I put another stick of wood in the stove, moved the enamel coffee pot to the hottest place, and poured in some more water. The coffee would likely be strong enough to walk out of the pot by itself.

I didn't know what to say to the curled up woman on the bed and I didn't know how PeeDee was doing, a dead man in her yard, and who knows what was happening to her Daddy. Maybe he was already in jail or hiding out somewhere.

I took two heavy white cups and filled them with coffee.

"Aunt Mattie, here's something for you to drink." I set the cup on the little table next to the bed. I delivered the other to the deputy who was leaning against the porch railing, looking down the dark road. He'd lit a lantern and hung it from a nail near the door.

"How soon they going to get electricity out here?" he grumbled.

I wanted to ask him about PeeDee, but my duty was with my aunt. Besides, he wouldn't have told me anything.

Addie and Ruth, the two women from the church, arrived before Uncle Cade's body. They hurried up the porch and into the house and then slowed down in respect for a death in the family.

"Ah, Lordy, what a fateful day this is," Addie said. "How much can one body stand?" She sat on the side of the bed and waited for Aunt Mattie to open her eyes. I knew they were thinking not only of Uncle Cade but of his and Aunt Mattie's boy, Nyle, as well.

They set me to work. I had to carry more water in, put a cloth on the table, stoke up the fire, and sweep. They were busy too. Aunt Mattie allowed herself to be helped into the bedroom where she discarded her apron and put on a Sunday dress. I heard the murmur of the women's voices with her and then she began to cry, harsh ragged weeping.

Addie came out and saw me standing motionless. "It'll do her good to let it out," she said. "Where does she keep the coffee? This brew'd make the very devil frown. You best get some milk from the spring house. May be some people here with babies to feed." I went to the front porch and took the lantern.

"Have to go get some milk," I told the deputy.

"Here, I'll carry that." I followed him down the steps. Then he carried the gallon jar of milk back to the house and let me swing the lantern.

"What happened at the Rednells?" I just needed to know.

"Old Man Rednell—drunker than a—I don't know exactly what went on. Sheriff Geer was dead when I got there. Right at the front door. Everybody quiet by then. Mrs. Rednell'd put a blanket over him. Don't look good for Rednell." That was a long speech for Alvin Jones and I could tell I'd get no more out of him. Still, I tried another question.

"Was everybody there, all the family?"

"Well, now, young'un, that's official business."

UNCLE CADE'S BODY was brought to the house and it stayed there until the next afternoon. Then the preacher convinced Mattie to let the funeral home in Sylva come and get it. So many people would want to be at the viewing and all, he said, better to let it be in town. So the black hearse came and took the body.

On that first night, though, twenty or twenty-five people dropped by. Some stayed until midnight and after. Addie and Ruth made Aunt Mattie go to bed finally and they stayed through the night. Taking turns dozing. I couldn't sleep. A few days in a new home and my first night with a dead body in the same house. I went to bed, still in my dress, but pretty soon I got up and crept back to the living room.

Uncle Cade was on a rough table the men had made. They'd laid boards, two wide chestnut boards, across a pair of sawhorses. He'd promised Aunt Mattie a corner cupboard from those boards. I'd heard him. The women had put a sheet on that and had placed a new Dresden Plate quilt over the body. They'd also put a clean shirt on him but hadn't tackled the job of getting his boots off. Dull pennies covered his eyes. His thinning hair was smoothed down. His skin was grayish and his jaw was kind of slack.

"Don't touch him, June," one of the women lurking around said. I thought she didn't have anything to do but watch me and everybody else. I wasn't about to touch him. I tried to remember Uncle Cade running down the porch steps a few hours earlier, but he was gone forever. Laid out stiff on that table is the way I'd remember him.

People stood around, talking now and then. Keeping their voices low. A few men wandered in and out. Mostly they stayed outside, even though it was chilly for late April. They came in to get warm, standing with backsides to the fireplace, rubbing their hands, commenting on the weather, President Roosevelt's death, the Rednells, the terrible deed. Then they wandered back outside.

One of the women said, "Guess they've got something out there to help keep'em warm." Others nodded.

"Did you get Mattie to take anything?" Addie whispered to her friend as they sliced pound cake in the kitchen.

"Not a drop. Even the doc told her she needed something for her nerves."

"My nerves died back yonder," Aunt Mattie had said. "I'll be all right now."

It was amazing to me that within a few hours, women could have cooked up and delivered so much food. Cobblers, pumpkin and apple pies, fried chicken, pans of biscuits and cakes of cornbread, green beans and pinto beans, potato salad, pickled beets and pickled corn lined the table and the back of the stove. Even deviled eggs. And people kept prodding others to eat. Nobody wanted to load up their plates, it being way past supper time.

But a few, disclaiming any hunger, did sample the goods. Mrs. Owenby, bent and haggard as a witch, protested a little and ate a lot, protested and ate some more. It was no secret she often went hungry if friends didn't stop in to leave a thing or two. Her no-good sons tended to forget her and she couldn't walk to a grocery store and didn't have any money anyway. Once her garden had run out and she'd finished her strings of leather britches and crocks of kraut and pickled beans and corn, she lived mostly on good will and generous neighbors. Nobody begrudged her the pleasure she took in the food and they urged her on. Eating kept us occupied, that and tending to the fire.

Of course, some people talked about what had happened and what would happen. But neighbors and friends were particularly careful of Aunt Mattie's feelings. To discuss the killing openly would be callous. Besides, no one knew much about it—or if they did, they weren't talking. Dr. Garret kept

9

silent and didn't stay very long when he delivered the body and checked on Aunt Mattie. And questions about my presence were few and quickly answered. Nobody seemed overly surprised that I was there.

"She's staying here now," Aunt Mattie said. I stood beside her rocking chair.

"Go keep warm by the fire, child," she told me. It was like there was a space around Aunt Mattie that she didn't want occupied by any living soul. I alternated between the fireplace and the front porch. The talk out there was a notch or two louder than in the living room, and the talk out in the yard near the tool shed was a notch or two louder than on the porch.

When the men noticed me in the shadows, they said less and took puffs on their Lucky Strikes and Camels. I heard one man mutter, "Damn shame Cade didn't have electricity put in 'fore now."

"Heard it was Mattie didn't want it," another said. After awhile they all quit talking till I wandered back in to the fire.

Out by the woodshed, Tommy Dotson played his harmonica, starting and stopping the mournful song that forever brought tears to my eyes because it was so sad: "Two little children, a boy and a girl stood by the old church door...clothes tattered and torn." Now, it seemed even sadder. If I was going to be left behind by Mama and Daddy, I wished, fleetingly, for a brother, for someone to share the questions with. I wished PeeDee was here. I went back into the house and opened the door to Aunt Mattie's bedroom, just to be sure she was there.

The Apple of Her Eye

As I TIPTOED around Aunt Mattie's grief and silence, the house seemed full of loss, loss past and present. Their only child, the boy Nyle, dead four years before and now his daddy.

Even before I went to live with her, I knew people thought Aunt Mattie was maybe a little odd. For one thing she and my uncle had only one child. That was sort of strange unless there was a medical problem, like maybe the woman had "female problems."

Mattie was young enough to have half a dozen more kids—or try to. That's what people said, "Looks like she'd want to fill up that awful void."

"T'aint fair to Cade," I heard an old busybody say one Decoration Day. "She ought to keep a-trying no matter if it kills her."

The preacher's wife snapped back at her, "I guess Cade Geer knows what he wants in this world."

In fact, Aunt Mattie'd lost two babies but she wasn't the type to advertise the fact. My mother told me the day they left me behind. Aunt Mattie'd been alone both times, she said, and almost bled to death the second time. Mama seemed angry then, snapping out the words.

"Don't you ever mention Nyle to your aunt. And don't go asking her why she don't have any more kids. Don't you ever mention it to anybody." I nodded. We had stopped to use the bathroom at the one gas station in Dillsboro between our house and the Geers.

"Not even Daddy?" I didn't understand the look that crossed her face. She knew I wouldn't be seeing Daddy—or her—anytime soon after that day. I wish she'd told me. No, I guess it was better to let the truth seep into my soul, kind of like water does more good if it seeps in slowly instead of coming in a flood and washing away the topsoil.

Mattie's son, Nyle, was the apple of her eye, her pride and joy. He was killed at the sawmill when he was eight.

I'd seen Nyle a few times. He had Uncle Cade's broad forehead with a cowlick to one side. His eyes were blue, widely spaced, his hair blond. His second grade school picture showed him in a plaid shirt and a solemn expression. He'd refused to smile because his front tooth was out.

I wasn't there so what I'm telling now is patched together from the various pieces and threads that I picked up between his awful accident and the time I got his room with his baseball bat still in the corner.

Nyle might have been more protected than most kids. Aunt Mattie constantly cautioned him about not diving in the dangerous end of the swimming hole and just about everything.

Naturally Nyle took to danger like ducks take to water, according to Mama. He allowed Old Man Baker to practice his knife throwing tricks on him, for example. Old Man Baker claimed he'd been in the circus and was a knife throwing expert. Since he told so many versions of his life before he turned up in Jackson County, people weren't sure what to believe. But he could throw a mean knife. He was bragging one day about the courage of his circus partner who stood still as a cricket with its head bit off while Baker surrounded him with a dozen knives. The boys clustered around Baker, both awed and skeptical, taunted the old man. He finally lost his patience.

"If'n there's a boy among you who'll put your head when your mouth is, I'll show you a thing or two." He was sharpening the beautiful hunting knife he carried in a sheath at his belt. It shone silvery in the sunlight. The boys blustered and retreated at the old man's words. Nyle, the quietest of the batch, took him up on the challenge.

"Show me what you can do, then," he said. Nyle must have believed Old Man Baker had been a circus knife thrower. He saw the respect with which the man treated his knife and the steadiness of his hand when he sharpened it. Other times, after a beer or something stronger, the hand was not so steady.

Old Man Baker looked long at Nyle. Of all the boys, Nyle was his favorite. Nyle was the one he sometimes flipped his cigarette butt to when he knew all the boys wanted a draw at the end of the butt. And Nyle was the sheriff's boy. He flipped the cigarette into the nearest mud puddle where it sizzled a second. The eyes of the boys followed it. Except Nyle. He kept his blue eyes on Baker. Baker shook his head. "Nah, boy. It ain't worth the risk."

The boys perked up. Nyle grinned and wiped his hands on his overalls. "Like you said, put up or shut up." It was an impudent speech for Nyle, who had been taught to respect his elders. "Come on, show your stuff. I'll stand right here in front of this tree."

Nyle stationed himself against the oak, small against its trunk. There were three inches on either side of his body. "Where you gonna put it?" It was a man-to-man confrontation. Old Man Baker saw there was no way out.

"Which side you partial to?" he asked. He backed up from the oak twenty paces. The boys moved to each side of the tree, elbowing each other a little.

With his right hand Nyle pointed to the side of his left cheek. "Put it there," he said.

Old Man Baker stood straight, ramrod straight. His thin white hair moved slightly in the breeze. Nothing else stirred. He wiped his knife on a white handkerchief and then rubbed it against his thigh. He held it out straight in front and sighted over it at his target. Nyle didn't seem to breathe. The boys said it was over before they got the real flavor of it. In an instant, and in one smooth movement, Baker drew back his arm and the knife was two inches from Nyle's left cheek. It hit with a thunk and quivered. They said Nyle didn't even turn pale, but Old Man Baker did. He walked toward the boy and Nyle met him half way. They shook hands the way men do, except Nyle hardly came up to his waist.

"Don't you boys ever doubt me agin," Baker said. They stood looking at the knife embedded in the oak. Not one dared touch it. Baker had to use all his strength to pull it out.

Anyway Nyle was barely six then and he was a known risk taker.

The sawmill drew him like morning glories draw bees or tobacco juice draws out a sting. He couldn't stay away. If Aunt Mattie had known how many times he went there without her permission she'd have fainted. He was absolutely forbidden from going there without an adult, and Nyle was generally obedient. Some man was always headed toward the sawmill and Nyle tagged along. The heavy logs, the whine of the belt, the shrillness of the cut—they drew the boy without mercy.

Everybody knew sawmills were dangerous places, places where man's commonsense came up against the will of the machine. The men who ran them knew their equipment and knew their boundaries; timing off a split second could mean a lost thumb, a sliced hand, or worse. Men didn't just go to work at the sawmill. They grew into it, absorbed the atmosphere, drank in the methodical movement, the watchful eye, the squint-eyed concentration of the long-time saw mill man. They didn't come apart at the sight of blood, their own or their friend's. They mastered the quick tourniquet, the quick step, the quick hand or they lost.

Nyle was a smart boy. He'd dare almost anything, but he had been bred to be watchful. He watched his step and he escaped a lot of silly childhood scars that the rest of us accumulated like battle medals. We got our necks scratched by the barbed wire we were creeping under and bled on our collars. We stumbled into a yellow jackets' nest and swelled up like thunderclouds out of the west; we'd catch a briar across the face in the fields or get a bat slung at our heads at school. Nyle went home from rock fights unscathed and from wrestling bouts unbloodied. If we'd thought about it, we might have said he led a charmed life.

Until the day they carried him to the truck, smashed, they said, almost beyond recognition. He was at the sawmill, watching, behaving himself. One minute he was standing out of the way, his eyes following the log as it traveled the belt, mesmerized by the whine of the belt. The next minute Mr. Young heard the rumble of the logs pyramided at the side of the yard. A chain had secured them. A link must have snapped. The first log probably killed Nyle, but they kept tumbling down. Mr. Young turned off the belt the second he heard the ominous rumble. He said it's like the clouds were grumbling at first. The other men came running but all they could do was stay out of the way. The logs stopped when one got turned sideways and slowed the others. By then at least a dozen had flattened Nyle. I didn't go to the funeral or to the graveyard, either, being too young, Daddy said. They didn't open the casket for viewing. They said the white lilies just blanketed the coffin and one girl fainted from the very smell of them. Mama took me with her to Mattie and Cade's house where I was supposed to stay out of the way. When everybody came back from the burying, the crowd was quiet. The women had laid out the food on the kitchen table, loads of it. People milled around. In the back bedroom I sat on the floor, not wanting to try to get onto the bed where three babies were sleeping. I heard Mrs. Duffey say to some other woman when they looked in to check on the babies, "It's almost more than a body can bear."

After a while a kind of wailing started. I don't know who started it, but soon a rhythmic lamentation set in. Even the men were saying mournful things: "Ah, Lord, I don't know. I don't know," "The lord help us, the lord help us all," "It's a terrible thing." And the women sounded a higher note so that a kind of sing-song cadence is what filled the house, not the words but the wavering sounds. After awhile, several women started just plain crying. Husbands went to their weeping wives and led them to chairs. Uncle Cade sat bent forward in a rocking chair on the front porch, his head between his hands. Aunt Mattie, who was sickly glaze-eyed, did not cry as two women led her to the bedroom.

Aunt Mattie didn't come out of her house, they said, for almost three months. But Uncle Cade got a summons the very next day to go break up a family fight two coves over. He had to get back to work. Aunt Mattie seemed normal when I saw her in church the next Christmas, thin, pale, a washed-out toughness to her, like a washrag that's been cloroxed too many times. But she was speaking to people and had her hymn book open even if she wasn't singing.

THE FIRST SUMMER ON BRUTON'S MOUNTAIN

Meeting PeeDee

MEETING PEEDEE WAS the biggest event in my life up till the day Mama and Daddy left me with Aunt Mattie. I knew then I wanted her for a best friend no matter what. I was seven going on eight that summer and had finished the first grade. Mama and Daddy had argued about me again. Daddy said, "She's awful young," but Mama insisted I was old enough to stay with Daddy's folks for a few weeks. They lived way back off the main road, up on Bruton's Mountain.

We didn't have a car, but somebody gave us a ride and let us out beside the highway a few miles from Glenville. We walked up the dirt road for what seemed like miles but was not quite two. Still, it was practically straight up, with some curves and "round the bends" thrown in. We passed only three houses.

The first house at the bottom of the mountain was fairly close to the highway. Ham and Flo lived there. We always stopped to visit before going on to Grandma and Grandpa Bruton's. According to Aunt Mattie, Flo had let herself go after their only daughter had run off and shamed herself. Flo was really fat and she moved slowly, lumbering on tiny feet that stuck out to the sides instead of pointing straight ahead. People said she had "sugar," like her weight wasn't her fault, that God had given her a burden she couldn't help. She kept sweets everywhere, sticks of store-bought peppermint candy, pies and apple cakes, and, once in a while, a big pan of fudge.

16

People got a sad note in their voices when they mentioned her. "Poor Flo, her sugar's bad. She's been going into them comas lately. Out of her head sometimes. She's gonna fall one of these days and not be able to get up." I marveled that she could heave herself out of the big chair in their living room and plod into the kitchen. Her kitchen smelled of sweat and cinnamon when she was baking, and Flo was generous. She'd wrap a fried apple pie in wax paper and tuck it into my pocket or give me a stick or two of striped candy. "Take that to tide you over, young'un. It's a long walk up that road."

The other houses between the highway and Grandpa and Grandma's place belonged to two brothers. They were cousins of Daddy's, so far removed that nobody bothered to explain exactly how we meshed with them, but they were family. On each trip to the mountain, we stopped to visit with them, and I'd get to play with the four or five kids at each place.

Jude and Louise's house was sort of on stilts, so we could go under the house in bad weather while the grownups talked. There were cracks in the floor, so we'd peek upwards once in a while. The sight of underwear sent us into giggles, and one of the grownups would yell, "You young'uns get out from under there. Get on out to the barn to play." We liked the dry bareness under the house, with all the cast-off junk and pieces of tools. We shared the space with three mangy hounds and some dusty chickens. The house was built on a hillside, so we girls had a hard time playing jacks on the slanted space, but we tossed pocket knives or just wrestled. One of the boys had a homemade banjo that he plucked. His one tune was "Wildwood Flower." This set of cousins didn't take much to schooling or reading. They mostly stayed out of their daddy's way. He was mean.

The other smaller house about half a mile on up the mountain belonged to the younger of the two brothers, Robert. Mama said that when their daddy died without a will, Jude, the mean brother, just took the better land and beat Robert until he signed whatever paper was put in front of him. Turned out, she said, Robert got a few scrubby acres without a good water supply. "Him and Jude don't get along to this day. You be careful you don't say nothing to get them fighting again." So I didn't talk about one set of cousins to the other. Sometimes the two sets of kids met, of course, but they didn't seem to want to start anything.

Annie and Robert's house sat flat on the ground, so it wasn't as interesting, having no playground under it. It was papered with newspapers and pages from catalogs and was warmer than Jude's place. Annie was quiet. I never heard her raise her voice to her children. That summer right after my eighth birthday, Annie had another baby. The oldest boy was eleven, Sue was nine, and the twins, Beth and Blanche, were almost five, Nan almost four. I liked to stop there because they had books in their house.

"They don't have running water," Daddy said one time, "but that Annie's got to have her books."

"And why not," my mother said. "What's she supposed to do stuck up there with Robert gone most of time, working in Gastonia, and no way to get out of there. A woman can't live on nothing but work and babies."

I noticed my daddy didn't say anything. Mama didn't like a lot of people, but she liked Annie. If we got to Bruton's Mountain early in the day, they'd sit for an hour or two, shelling beans or peeling apples, talking and drinking coffee. Mama talked more to Annie than to anybody. Daddy sat on the front porch if Robert wasn't there. I would go off with Sue, and we'd read or try to read her mother's Doubleday Book Club books. I read the walls, too. They weren't the only newspapered walls I'd seen, but they were the best. Sue said her daddy brought home the newspapers from the city and they just kept adding them to the walls. That house was real snug.

Annie didn't usually have any sweets to give me, but once she gave me a penny. She said it came from Gastonia and it had been run over and squashed by a train on its way to New Orleans. I loved that "lucky penny." I carried it with me all one year, and then I must have lost it in the blackberry field. I mourned for days.

The road from the highway up to Jude's and on to Robert's was bordered much of the way by cleared land, pastures with barbed wire fences propped up or falling down, and even a little stand of apple trees, Winter Johns and Limber Twigs mostly, that never did much good.

After Robert's place, though, the road was not so steep, but it got darker and more closed in. The road wound through laurel and rhododendron bushes that grew right to the edge, some jutting out over the road. Even in the summer, a feeling of dampness hung over the road as if the bushes never totally dried out. Sometimes little rivulets of water crossed the road and followed its curves. Grandpa used a sled for hauling logs down the mountain, so we had pretty good ruts to walk in. We paid attention along the sides for snakes and avoided the higher grass in the middle. We had to wade two little creeks between Robert's and Grandpa's place. I poked around in the shallow water under the rocks for crawdads and lizards while Mama and Daddy rested.

I guess Daddy looked forward to seeing his folks. We visited two or three times a year, but until the summer I met PeeDee, my feet got heavier the closer we got to their house. Mama'd turn around to see me a few feet behind and yell, "Come on, June. We ain't got all day. We want to be out of here before dark. Hurry up."

As we rounded the last curve before the open pasture and garden, Daddy always yelled, "Hey, it's Carl."

Once I asked Flo why my daddy always stopped and yelled out his name, why didn't we just go on into the clearing. She paused for a fraction in shaping the pie crust. "A precaution, June. Your grandpa don't take to people coming in on him unannounced."

This time as we approached, I tugged at Daddy's sleeve. "Pre-Caution," I said.

"Huh?" Daddy looked surprised, and then his shy grin lit up his face. "Ain't you something! Precaution."

Daddy yelled again and Mama called out, "Hey, Mrs. Bruton," and told me, "Say hello to your Granny now."

Grandma came out to meet us. She was a stout woman, resigned-faced, slightly stooped. Her gray hair was in a coiled bun. She dipped snuff, like most grandmas did. So did Grandpa when he didn't have a chew of tobacco. Grandma didn't smile much, maybe a touch of a smile passed over her face when we first appeared in the clearing.

"Hey, Grandma," I dutifully greeted her. She had on a clean apron by the time we got to the porch because the dogs barking had already alerted her to company. Except for funerals I didn't ever see her without an apron. In its pocket she kept her Dental Sweet snuff, a little pocket knife with an ivory handle, some safety pins, and a handkerchief. I especially liked the little pocketknife even after she used it one day to pick a splinter from the fleshy part of my hand. Mostly she used it to cut a "toothbrush" from a sassafras bush to chew on as she worked.

Grandpa and Grandma Bruton's house was gray. The barn was gray and they were gray. The rocks at the edge of the yard were gray and mossy, and a hundred yards or so beyond the house was a gray sheet of rock. Everybody called it the rock cliff. It just came down out of the woods above, straight down. Under it was a wet, mossy area. I wasn't allowed to play near it. The grownups always warned, "Don't go over to the cliff. If you crawl back in there, we'd never get you out." The place fascinated me. Naturally, I sneaked over to the cliff and stretched out on my stomach and tried to see under it. It was scary. I really wouldn't crawl back in there. Not more than two feet separated the end of the cliff and the ground, and it was coal black dark under there.

FOR A FEW DAYS, I was lonely at Grandpa and Grandma Brutons. Grandma even came and sat on my bed a couple of nights till I went to sleep. The only one of their children still at home was Uncle Johnnie, a morose fourteen-year-old. Johnnie hadn't gone to school much, Daddy said, because he never could learn to read. Mama said, "He may be slow, but he's their baby boy, and your pa wants him kept at home to help out." Daddy answered, "He's too old now to go back, long as the school forgets him."

PEEDEE CAME RIDING into my life on the back of Johnnie's old mare, Odd. He had been over the mountain at the Watsons. He got home around four, a girl behind him. I was sitting on the back porch steps, watching a stream of ants coming and going.

She had blond pigtails, rather messily braided, and blue eyes. A few freckles ran across her nose. In one swift movement she slid off Odd's back and announced, "I'm Prudence Delilah Rednell, nine and a half. Everybody calls me PeeDee. I've come to play with you."

Johnnie mumbled, "Her family's living on the Watsons' place this summer, helping out." He turned to lead the horse toward the barn. "Told her you was here. She's bound and determined to come visit."

"Well, hey." I guess I was grinning because I could certainly use some company, but for the moment, the cat had got my tongue, and I couldn't think of anything to say.

"We're poor," Prudence Delilah said. "But I brought you something." She pulled a piece of red ribbon from her pocket. "My secret pal give it to me at the Christmas party at school last year. You can have it."

She stood with her hands on her hips, surveying the green and gray farm, surveying me. She was at least a head taller. Her eyes sparkled as if in approval.

"What's your name?" She nodded toward Johnnie's retreating figure. "He said you was here, but he didn't say your name. He don't talk much, does he?"

"I'm June," I said. "Let's go look at Grandma's grapevines." I held the ribbon with a certain reverence. I, too, had pigtails, dark brown and not quite as long as hers. "This color'd look

CELIA H. MILES

better on your head than mine." I meant it, but I hoped she wouldn't offer to take the ribbon back.

"Nope. It's yours. Here, let me tie it on." She gave a slight tug of my braids. "I'll just put it on this one pigtail. You're lopsided now!"

We giggled and ran off to investigate what might be called Grandma's one vanity, her new grapevines. She'd swapped three gallons of molasses to Lisabeth Sams for their start years earlier, and finally the vines were twining around the wires Johnnie had strung between the poles. Lots of fox grapes grew throughout the mountain, especially along the streams, not cultivated and cared for. I liked the tartness and tang of the fox grapes, but Grandma's grape arbor was a special place for me. I liked to watch Grandma tenderly tie the vines to train them along the wires. Her roughened fingers treated the vines with a gentleness I longed for from my mama.

My new friend was properly impressed with the arbor and pronounced it downright pretty. She touched one of the hard green grapes. "Can't you just taste it already?"

Johnnie must have told Grandma that I had a visitor, for she didn't come out to check on me or holler for me as she usually did. She didn't want me wandering too far by myself. When we finally trudged into the kitchen at supper time, she'd set a plate for PeeDee.

"Get washed up, you two. Lord, what mud puddle did you find this time?"

"This is Prudence Delilah Rednell, but everybody calls her PeeDee," I said. "Can she spend the night?"

"What kind of name is that," grumbled my Grandma, busy with ladling up stewed potatoes and frying fatback. She nodded yes to my question before I went on, "Johnnie said they said she could stay."

I felt important, having a friend all my own. And I was proud that Grandma took special pains to pass PeeDee seconds on everything, which she ate steadily. Grandpa and Johnnie

22

didn't seem to take in how different I felt, but I could tell they noticed my red ribbon.

The next morning PeeDee and I carried water for Grandma, filled up the wood box, and swept the whole house. When she told us to get out from under her feet, she had work to do, PeeDee and I headed straight for the gray cliff. The grass near the cliff was damp and squishy beneath our bare feet. I stopped about five feet from the cliff.

"This is as far as I'm supposed to go." Grandma had told me to stay back of a little clump of laurel, stunted, that grew on a flat stone that jutted through the soil. It had accumulated enough dirt to sustain that little bush, and it had ridges along with little potholes where rainwater pooled. I sat on the warm stone, looking at the dark underside of the cliff. PeeDee scratched her name on the gray stone with a piece of quartz and collected a pile of tiny white pebbles. They weren't anywhere near as big as marbles. I wondered how those little pebbles got there. After a while, we both stared at the darkness under the cliff.

"I could crawl back in under there," PeeDee said. "It'd get my dress awful dirty, but I could do it."

"You couldn't see a thing," I said. "You might not come back out if you got stuck or something." Just the thought sent a chill up my spine. But I was curious.

"Come on, let's go look," she said. We crept closer, like Indians sneaking up on cowboys, almost tiptoeing. The house seemed a long way off.

A dank odor seeped out from the cliff. The ground was colder, too. Here it was in July and my feet were freezing. Right at the opening, we both squatted down and peered into the darkness. PeeDee seemed less sure of crawling under there, or maybe she was considering the consequences. I hoped she wouldn't ask me to crawl in with her. I'd have to do it, and I knew I would do it, especially if she dared me, but I didn't want to. I poked around in a large log that lay half rotted in the dark soil. The tree had come up by the roots, in a storm, I guess, and part of it had been sawed off and probably used for firewood. The roots had moss and some little starflowers growing among them, and the rest of the tree was rotting.

"Look at these flowers," I directed PeeDee, hoping to postpone what was sure to be inevitable. I saw a squirming nest of wormy looking creatures. "Hey, look in there!"

"Them's little snakes," she said. "I never saw such little snakes. Babies, I reckon."

I was watching all the tiny eyes. They kept moving like the black dots you can get when you squeeze your eyelids shut tight.

"Let's keep them," PeeDee said. "You run get a jar to put'em in."

"I don't know," I said doubtfully. "They could be poisonous."

"No, they're not. Run. I'll stay here and keep them in this stump-hole." PeeDee looked at me. "Unless you want me to get a jar and you stay here."

I ran back to the house. Grandma's canning jars were in a sort of half basement, under the kitchen porch. I grabbed a green half gallon jar with a lid and raced back to the cliff.

PeeDee was guarding the snakes, a stick in her hand. "They're just sweet little babies," she said.

They didn't look too sweet to me. I'd been told a thousand times to watch out for snakes, and even snakes not much bigger than these were dispatched with a hoe or a rock by any adult who saw them. But I had not seen any this small and so many of them twisting together. I guess they hadn't tried to get out of the nest.

I held the jar next to the hole, and PeeDee tried to rake the snakes into the opening. She concentrated, muttering, "Go on in, you little snake, go on in." When four or five were in the jar, the others were freer to squirm away from PeeDee's stick.

"Shucks," she said, "I'll show them." In a flash, she dropped the stick, stuck her hand into the hole, and picked up the remaining three snakes. For a moment she held them in the air, squirming in her fist. Then she plunked them in the jar and

I got the lid on. My knees were shaking so bad I had to sit down on the dry stone. That jar was alive with fury.

"That—that was something," I stuttered. "That was awful brave, picking them up with your bare hand."

"That was stupid," she said. "But once I make up my mind, I'll do anything."

We sat for a long time, watching our captured snakes. They had been more interesting to me in their own nest. They thrashed and slithered inside that greenish-blue jar, and even though I knew they couldn't unscrew that lid from the inside, I was reluctant to pick up the jar. The more I looked at it, the uglier it became. "What we going to do with them?"

"Take them back to show to Johnnie and your folks. Likely Johnnie's never caught him any snakes."

"I bet there's all kind of snakes under that cliff. That's probably the home base for all the snakes on this mountain. I bet there's hundreds under there." Looking into that darkness I thought I could see shapes and eyes in there.

"It's dinnertime," PeeDee said. "Let's go eat." For a thin girl she had a terrific appetite. "I'll carry the jar."

I was glad she volunteered. I couldn't have picked it up. She carried it straight out in front of her, both hands on the lid.

Grandpa and Johnnie were home for the noon meal and already sitting at the table. We thought we'd better leave the snake jar outside, so we placed it on the washstand on the back porch. The washstand was a rough shelf where the water buckets sat, along with a shallow round pan for washing our hands. We stood on tiptoes splashing our hands, using the slick bar of soap still damp from the menfolks' hands, soap Grandma had made last fall. The jar sat slightly above my eye level. So far, even without oxygen, the little snakes were still writhing around. When we sat down, my stomach didn't feel too settled, but I managed to eat the fried potato cakes and hot cornbread, with just a little helping of beans. PeeDee kept glancing toward the back door, but she hadn't lost her appetite.

25

When Grandpa got up and left the table, I had my mouth completely full of cornbread and sweet milk. I couldn't say a word before he was out the back door.

"God dang! What in thunder's them snakes doing here! Woman! June!" We had some explaining to do, and we did. Grandma didn't come out on the porch. She stood in the doorway, eyeing the jar.

"Look at the markings there. You can see they're copperheads. Poison as the day is long. Didn't you have enough sense to see they weren't blacksnakes?" At Grandpa's words, Grandma wrung her hands in her apron folds and shook her head in amazement.

Grandpa's cold voice and frown put me in my place. I'd be in disgrace for the rest of the summer, I reckoned.

"Get your shotgun, Johnnie," he said. "Nah, get us a couple of hoes."

He didn't intend to blast a perfectly good half gallon jar to pieces. PeeDee and I stood back a respectful distance. After Johnnie poured the snakes out, he and Grandpa methodically chopped their heads off. While they had seemed so snakey-mean in the jar, I felt sorry for them, dumped on the hard ground, no chance to wiggle off into the grass, sluggish as they were by then. I even felt my eyes dampen. But I didn't let Grandpa see that.

The two went toward the rock cliff. Johnnie carried his gun and Grandpa took the hoe, because as Grandma said, "They's bound to be a mother snake out there. Lord help us, likely more than one."

PeeDee and I started to follow, staying far back, but Grandpa looked around and with one motion of his hand sent us back to the house. We washed the dishes, and Grandma set us to filling the wood box even though it was earlier than usual for that chore. I wish she hadn't said, as she usually did, "Now, look out for snakes." We were sitting on the steps in the sun, drawing on our arms with pokeberry juice, when we heard the shot.

In a few minutes Grandpa and Johnnie appeared with a brown snake, head smashed, still wiggling on the hoe handle. "Biggest copperhead I've seen around here," Grandpa said.

Johnnie stretched it out, and it was as long as the hoe handle. Grandma told him to dump the snake at the edge of the yard, the usual spot. Its corpse was supposed to deter other snakes from crossing over into our territory. I think it worked. Except for a resident black snake that liked the window sill of the back bedroom for sunning and a garter snake or two every summer, I didn't see any snakes near the house ever again.

We washed the canning jar in the leftover dishwater and left it on the washstand. A day or so later Grandma said it accidentally got knocked off and broke. I didn't blame her. I wouldn't want to eat anything canned in that jar.

PeeDee stayed with us almost a week before her family told Johnnie to bring her back across the mountain. I thought I'd never see her again, and I cried myself to sleep a couple of nights. We promised to write, but we wouldn't have stamps to mail our letters with. Daddy might mail mine, but PeeDee told me her dad would not waste any money on postage.

Maybe in answer to my unspoken prayers, PeeDee's family moved in November and PeeDee and I went to the same school. PeeDee's oldest brother out in Seattle lost a leg in a railroad accident and got some money settled on him. He sent it so the family could buy a run-down house and some acreage over in Mooney's Cove. Because her family had moved around so much when she started to school, PeeDee was behind and we were in the same grade.

Our Days Go By

WHEN PEEDEE WAVED goodbye and returned to help her family farm the Watsons' place, I didn't have anyone to play with and I missed her. Grandma said I was a big help with chores, but I was lonely for PeeDee.

With just Grandpa and Johnnie at home, and me in the summertime, Grandma kept busy. I couldn't imagine how she managed when all her children were there. They were scattered all around now. The oldest boy, L.R., was gone. Two, William and Jordon, were in the army, somewhere in Italy or Germany. Daddy had been rejected because of flat feet. Two daughters, Leonie and Evelyn, lived in the Piedmont, near Gastonia or High Point. They worked in big factories and didn't come home, even for Christmas. Another daughter, Little Beth, had died of the scarlet fever when she was seven. Daddy said her grave was way up on the mountain, not in a regular graveyard with a church close by. Now, Grandma couldn't walk that far it was so steep. Daddy was, besides Johnnie, the closest to his parents in terms of geography, but I think L.R. was closest in love.

L.R. had run away or had gotten into trouble with the law when he was around eighteen and hadn't been heard from since. Nobody talked about him. He was his mama's favorite boy, Daddy said, and it just about killed her when he took off. I looked at "Sunset over the Rockies" on the 1945 calendar and imagined L.R. roaming in those barren mountains, hunting cougars and grizzly bears. One rainy day when I was staring at the calendar and daydreaming about the uncle I'd never seen, I thought, "I bet Uncle L.R. is glad he's out there where the deer and the antelope roam." Grandma whipped her head around and I realized I'd said the words out loud. When I saw her face, I was sorry I'd spoken.

Grandma said, "Wherever he is, I hope he's happy." She was paring apples into salt water until we could put them out to dry. She sliced off half a peeled apple and handed it to me. "Here, child. This winesap's good." I had eaten two apples earlier while she was churning and wasn't hungry, but I took the offering.

"Thanks, Grandma." I went to the kitchen stove for salt to sprinkle on the apple.

Besides me and Johnnie and Grandpa, Grandma had other mouths to feed. A lone and skinny spotted cow, a Jersey, roamed behind the barn. Old Maybelle, Grandma called her. She managed to give a lot of milk out of her thin sides. Sometimes it tasted faintly of wild onions. Then Johnnie and I were ordered to get out to the pasture the next day and dig up all the wild onions. He had a regular hoe and I used a short handled hoe, its blade worn so thin it was bent in the middle. Digging wild onions in a rocky pasture was hard, but who wanted to drink oniony milk all summer.

Then there was Oscar the mule, gray and getting white around the ears he was so old. Why they kept him I don't know. I wanted to like Oscar, but there was nothing friendly about him. He let me get fairly close and then he'd lay his ears back and get wild-eyed. Sometimes we just looked, each taking the measure of the other. I wanted him to nuzzle me like he did Johnnie when Johnnie gave him an ear of corn. But he belonged to Johnnie and stayed well back from me.

The two big work horses, good for sledding logs or hauling produce in the wagon, were rough-coated but docile enough. Johnnie'd named them Odd and Even. Sometimes Johnnie swung me onto the back of Odd and led me around the edge of the pasture. Johnnie was good like that sometimes. Other times he just flat ignored me.

Grandma really liked her chickens, mostly Rhode Island Reds and Domineckers, with a mighty rooster to keep them company. I hated that rooster. He'd flog a person in a minute. Johnnie had to keep the chicken lot in good repair, but Grandma lost some chickens every summer to foxes or "mushrats" that lived below the clearing where the stream spread and puddled. If a favorite hen disappeared, Grandma set traps for the big rats and sometimes she caught one. Grandma was a gentle woman, but she'd take a big stick to anything after her chickens. She beat a possum to death when she caught it in the chicken pen. When I saw her smashing that possum, she looked surprised at herself and muttered, "They ain't civilized, possums ain't."

I thought about that and a few days later said, "Well, Grandma, the possums have to eat too."

"Not my chickens they don't, young lady."

When she called me "young lady," I knew I'd offended. I sat and thought about it a long time. I didn't like the looks of possums, ugly creatures, and I didn't like plump fluffy chickens either. I guessed whatever people could keep in a pen and protect and eat when they wanted to was the creature to be thankful for. Still it didn't make a lot of sense. Grandma liked her chickens and would protect them with a stick and a trap but they got eaten—by us. When the time came for chicken and dumplings, sometimes Johnnie would do it, but more often than not, Grandma grabbed up the unsuspecting chicken and wrung its neck with a twist and a snap. Then she chopped off its head and threw it over the edge of the yard, and picked the chicken clean, after dowsing its body in scalding water to loosen the feathers. She plucked the big feathers out and next got at the little pin feathers. It was a messy sight. Just getting a meal like chicken together took a lot of time. No wonder Grandma looked tired.

Besides Johnnie's big old dog named Lash, two cats lived at Grandma and Grandpa's. Tabby stayed close to the house and slept on the porch, often on the wash stand. The other was a tom cat. It roamed and prowled and fathered lots of kittens with Tabby. She was usually pregnant when I was there, but I never got to see the kittens born, and there weren't ever any kittens to pet when I arrived. When I asked, Grandma said she gave some of them to Louise or Annie. I don't know what happened to the others.

ROBERT SAID TO Daddy one time, "Don't nobody mess with your pa," and Daddy had nodded. Grandpa seemed all right to me, but he noticed me about as much more as he might a butterfly. Once I heard him raise his voice to Grandma, and it was scary. I'd gone to the spring for a bucket of water so I don't know what set him off. Grandma must have said something he didn't like. Grandpa's voice made little goose bumps raise up on my arms. "Don't ought me, woman!" Grandma didn't say anything else. When I plunked the bucket down, Grandma came into the kitchen and Grandpa went out the front door.

Grandpa always wore black. His hat was a kind of rounded "bowler" hat, not the slouchy felt hats most old men wore. Suspenders held up his wool pants and he didn't wear a belt. Most men I knew wore overalls or dark work pants, and teachers and preachers wore suits. Grandpa kept his black coat on most of the time, even in the summer, and his shirt was buttoned to the top. I never saw that top button undone on his shirt. On Sunday the shirt was white; other days, a gray or khaki color.

Most of the time Grandpa kept his hat on even in the house, except at the table. His hair was dirty gray. Grandma was his barber. After supper at least once each summer he stationed himself on the back porch and fastened a cloth about his shoulders. Grandma used a pair of clippers to trim his hair and neck. He didn't bother to even glance in the looking glass that stood on the washstand, at least not while I was watching. Maybe he checked out his haircut when he shaved the next morning.

Usually Grandma said, "Come here, Johnnie, might as well trim you while I'm at it," and Johnnie took the seat vacated by Grandpa. Johnnie sat very still. I think he enjoyed having his mother work on his head. Grandma was extra gentle with the clippers on Johnnie.

THE HOUSE ITSELF didn't take a lot of care. It was logs chinked with red clay around the back; the front part had rough boards nailed over the logs. The entire building had grayed into a somber spot in the green landscape. Gray shingles covered the roof, and a few were missing. When it rained, we put buckets or pans here and there, mostly in the back room, the older part of the house, where Johnnie slept. The kitchen floor was covered with linoleum, torn and rough around the edges. It was cool and gritty under my bare feet and greasy, too. The weekly mopping didn't have much effect on its barely visible greenish pattern.

Every Monday was wash day. Grandma's big black wash pot swung low to the ground from a bar across two big stumps in the backyard. Before the sun came up, Johnnie carried wood and placed it under the black pot, started the fire, and left the rest to us. From the spring, I carried water to fill the pot, buckets and buckets of it. While the fire heated the water, Grandma fed me biscuits and gravy and changed the beds. After we dumped the clothes and sheets in, I stirred with a long wooden paddle.

Mama had real detergent from the store, but Grandma used her homemade lye soap. She scrubbed the clothes on her washboard and held them up to be sure she'd not missed any stubborn dirt. Her hands must have had their nerve endings worn off long ago because she could wring out the clothes from the hot water and immerse them in the cold rinse water without flinching. I was good at carrying water and watching the fire, but I was a miserable failure at actually washing the clothes. I burned my fingers in the scalding water and could never wring the clothes dry enough to hang on the line.

"Takes lots of practice, June," Grandma said. "Don't you worry about it yet. You just take care of the water."

Electricity didn't come up the mountain beyond Flo's place. A kerosene lamp, its chimney darkened with soot, sat on the mantle of the fireplace. Another one stayed on the kitchen table or on the worktable. Normally we went to bed around dark, so as not to waste kerosene. When all their children had been home, the girls shared a bedroom, the boys one, and Grandpa and Grandma the other. Now I had my own room with a chest of drawers with three of its four drawers crammed with quilts, a straight chair, and a bed with a cornshuck mattress. We had a regular mattress at home, but I got used to the sounds and vegetable smell of corn shucks. Sometimes I heard noises coming from Grandma and Grandpa's room—cornshuck rustling and creakings and grunts and muffled sounds. Only a board wall separated the rooms. The same sort of sounds came from my parents' room, usually late at night when I was supposed to be asleep, only they were livelier, even without the sound of cornshucks.

My pillow was soft and downy, full of goose feathers. Grandma used to have geese, but Mama told me that they were messy creatures and wouldn't stay in their pen. After Grandpa stepped in their messings a couple of times, he told Grandma he'd better not see that goose grease in the yard anymore or that would be the end of the geese. She tried to keep them penned up, but without luck. When Grandpa came home after dark and slipped in the goose grease, he chopped the heads off the geese that very night. He made Johnnie hold the lantern while he did it. And he left the mess, bloody white bodies and heads flung here and there, in the yard. Grandma surely heard the commotion, the flappings, squawkings, and cursings, but she didn't get up to see.

The next morning she carried the dead geese by their feet, their bloody congealed necks dragging the ground, two at a time down the road a piece and threw them over the bank. That's where anything unusable or broken was thrown. Johnnie said wild animals or maybe hunting dogs probably carried them off and ate them. He said he'd see a soft white feather out in the woods for months after that.

One day I saw Grandpa's famous pistol. We had walked the four miles to the post office and store. I knew Grandma was tired when she just sat on the back porch. If Grandpa hadn't been sitting on the bed that morning, she'd never have gone off and left it unmade. Through their cracked bedroom door, I could see the rumpled bed covers. I went in and smoothed the top quilt and pulled the counterpane up. When I picked up a pillow, I saw a pistol, Grandpa's pistol. I knew he had one, but I didn't know he slept with it under his head. They said Grandpa's daddy had stolen it from a Yankee soldier boy that had been wandering around lost from his regiment when they came through the mountains. It looked awfully polished up to be that old. I stared at it and wondered whether to mess up the bed so Grandma wouldn't know I'd been in there or finish the chore. I decided to finish up.

"Grandma, I made up your bed," I said when I joined her later in the kitchen. "I saw Grandpa's pistol." She nodded.

"Does he always keep it there?"

"When it's not on him or on the chest of drawers," she said. "Best not mention it to him."

I didn't intend to mention it to him. Everybody knew the pistol went with Grandpa whenever he left the mountain, even to church. And to the schoolhouse, especially at voting time. Grandpa voted straight Republican. They said he kept his pistol in sight at the voting place, but as far as I know he never had to use it. Almost everybody voted Republican anyway and didn't need any persuading. Grandma didn't vote, it not seeming fitting, she said, for a woman to hang around the polling place. That was a man's place. Grandpa couldn't do anything about the fact that the woman schoolteacher sat at the table and marked off names, but he didn't like it.

The house seemed awfully quiet after PeeDee left. There wasn't a radio so I missed all my programs that I listened to at home. "Amos and Andy" I could do without, but "The Lone Ranger" and "Sky King of the Yukon" were like friends, and I wanted to know what they were doing.

Sometimes I wished the house had newspapered walls like Annie's instead of just the Bible and an almanac and a calendar on the living room wall. It didn't take me long to go through the months of the year, reading "Sunset over the Rocky Mountains," and "The Kentucky Derby" and "New England in the Fall." The almanac had some interesting stuff in it along with lots of little columns of figures and facts, but usually it was on the mantle, out of my reach. It was for the grownups to read. The Bible was a large dark tome. I never saw Grandpa read, but I think he could. The Bible had been heavily used, its cover worn thin at the edges from being turned. Sometimes in the early evening Grandma thumbed through it, stopping to scan a passage occasionally. She looked long minutes at the pages at the beginning where names of the family were written in, with birth dates and death dates. When she stopped at a page, her lips moved as she read.

Johnnie wasn't much company. He was just Johnnie. I read to him, and I noticed that Grandma listened. I don't know if Johnnie understood half what I read, certainly I didn't. He didn't care how I pronounced the names in the Bible. He'd listen and whittle. Once in a while, I ran out of breath stumbling over the words and just stopped. Johnnie didn't seem to notice. He whittled on, his big hands carefully shaping a ball within a chain link in the pine wood. The floor at his chair was always littered with wood shavings. He brushed off his overalls when he stood up, and the shavings drifted to the floor. Grandma swept them up every night before I took over that chore.

GRANDPA HAD A fiddle and on warm evenings if there was company, he might play a few tunes. Company was a special occasion. People just didn't visit the Brutons. That summer only two sets of company came.

One afternoon soon after PeeDee left, Mr. Watson and his boy from across the mountain rode over to borrow a wagon. Theirs had broken down and they had a load of corn to get out of the field and nobody to send to Sylva for a new axle and wheel.

I was sitting on the porch, drying my poison ivy, and must have looked a sight. The boy didn't look at me after the first sneaky grin at my discomfort. My eyes were swollen almost shut and my fingers oozed clear liquid. Johnnie had been clearing some new ground down the road and he must have burned some poison ivy and the smoke or fumes had gotten me. I kept clear of the stuff if I saw it. Grandma had mixed buttermilk and baking soda and smeared it on my hands. All day she'd said, "Don't scratch it. You'll spread it," and I tried hard. She'd just wiped my fingers and eyes with a cloth and dabbed more white paste on me.

Grandpa slipped something in a bag to Mr. Watson before they hitched the horses to the wagon. They asked him for a tune, and he took the fiddle from the wall where it hung and settled it under his chin. The boy brought the rocking chair out on the porch for Grandma and she rocked and rested and told me not to scratch.

"Play "Watch the Waters A-Gliding'," Grandma said. I liked the tune, and Grandpa played another one I didn't know. It made me feel dreamy and mournful, but Grandpa apparently wasn't satisfied as he laid the fiddle aside.

"I'm rusty as a bent nail," he complained.

"Right pretty, Mr. Bruton," the boy said. They sat on the floor, their backs against the house.

"Can you stay for supper?" Grandma asked. "Nothing fancy, but lots of it."

"Can't do it, ma'am. We done and eat, but thank you anyhow. We best get this wagon back across the mountain. You come see us sometime."

Grandma thanked them for asking and said she would.

"That boy has got the biggest two feet I've ever seen," I declared, "and both of them left."

"Is that any way to talk, young lady?"

"That's what Mama said about a neighbor boy," I said.

Grandma put her hands on her hips and looked at my hands. She didn't have to say another thing. I could just hear the boy describing my pasty ooziness.

I was pretty sure Grandma wouldn't go visiting the Watsons. She didn't go many places. To church in good weather. To the post office and store. She visited Flo at the foot of the mountain on her way back from other places. Sometimes Louise came out to the road and they talked. She did stop at Annie's to "rest before the going on" as she put it.

One time, Grandma paused to rest as we struggled up the road with some store bought stuff. "Lord, June, I's born and raised in these mountains, but I hope Heaven's got some flat land."

I nodded solemnly. I'd seen pictures of the beach and the desert, but I couldn't imagine a totally flat country. Being able to see that far would be scary in a way. I'd rather have something like a mountain or hill rear up and block out what must be big empty spaces. Still I spent hours imagining what might be over that mountain, and over that one, and over that one. Somewhere over one of them was the Piedmont and the ocean, and California was over in the other direction.

I didn't want to go back to the rock cliff after PeeDee left that first summer. But it did intrigue me. I'd just sit on the porch and look at it. The dark places of the world. What was back in there? I pictured Indian bones and dog bones and snake skins and even streaks of gold, veined and giving off a glow in the blackness. That rock cliff fed my imagination for hours and days on end.

One time Grandma caught me daydreaming. "What you doing, June?"

"Thinking about how far back that dark goes and all the bones in there."

"Lord, young'un, you ain't got enough to do around here. Come and help me string these beans."

Grownups didn't trust kids to do much thinking. Better to put their hands to work, because as someone was sure to say, "Idle hands is the devil's workshop."

Grandma canned at least one hundred half gallon jars of green beans in a good year, and the green beans that Grandma didn't can she strung up to dry as Aleather britches." We pulled the strings off and ran a needle with heavy white thread through each bean until the string was a yard or so long. Those strings were left to dry during the rest of the summer and into the winter. Then they'd be soaked overnight to soften them up and cooked all day with a piece of fatback. They'd be dark brown and limp, and all their dark specks showed. Grandma always sent a string or two home with us to eat with a winter onion and slaw or cooked cabbage and cornbread.

We also dried apples. Sometimes Grandma made applesauce or apple butter, stirring all day over a hot stove. Some women had big copper pots they'd cook the apples in, sometimes out in the yard. Grandma made hers in the kitchen and the whole house smelled of dark spices and stickiness. But she liked dried apples for fried pies and apple cakes. We cored and sliced apples and put them in salt water, then laid them out to dry, usually on a piece of tin set on a couple of sawhorses. I had to watch the cats and chickens to see they didn't investigate the drying apples. That was a time for more thinking. Sometimes I sat so long and so still I thought I could see a freckle growing right out of my arm.

Besides the Watsons, Jude came visiting, stayed for two or three hours. The two men leaned back on the porch in their straight chairs. They chewed tobacco and spit off the porch. With his pocket knife Jude trimmed his fingernails, digging under the nails to remove the dark line. Then he took out his whetstone and sharpened the knife. I drifted between the porch steps and the kitchen where Grandma was canning blackberries. Jude had set two gallon buckets on the table. "Louise sent these. She's got more than she can handle."

I heard a few scraps of conversation between the men's long silences.

Grandpa said, "Reckon them Rednells are still at the Watsons."

"Yep. Reckon so. Seen the oldest boy at the store last week."

"A man ought to have his own place, the way I see it."

Jude said, "Red Rednell drinks heavy, I hear. One of these days somebody's gonna clean his plow."

I wanted to hear more. PeeDee hadn't come right out and said her daddy was a drunk. I was glad she couldn't hear them. They didn't say anything else. After awhile I went back to the kitchen.

"Bring me a bucket of water, June," Grandma directed. "Pour it in that pot there."

I had eaten cooked sweetened blackberries swimming in butter for breakfast with big biscuits. And I'd eaten some more at noon. The sweet odor in the kitchen was overpowering, but I stayed and stirred and watched Grandma "put up" the berries. An hour later, I was back on the porch steps. The men hadn't changed their positions. But Jude's favorite hound which had not dared come straight to the house but had slunk around the yard had finally made his way to the shade under the porch. It lay curled in the dust.

"Jesse left day before yesterday," Jude said. He spat with some energy.

"Join the army?" Grandpa asked.

"Nope. Not as I know of. Just left." Jude wiped his stubbled cheek. "Gone before I got up, 'fore any of us was up. Told nobody. Walked to the highway. No sign of him coming back."

Jesse was thin as a candlewick, with a quick sideways grin. Daddy said that grin was going to get him in trouble one of these days—if not with the girls, he said, with his Daddy. Jude wasn't known for grinning. I didn't blame him. His teeth were yellowed and ugly and two had been broken in a fight. He barely opened his mouth when he talked and he didn't talk much.

"Courting?" That was Grandpa.

"Not that I know of. Next thing we'll hear is he's in trouble or in the army, I guess." Jude shrugged. "One less mouth to feed."

From what I'd gathered from Mama and Daddy, Jesse had done most of the work around the place, kept the chicken lot repaired, plowed in the spring and got the crops in.

"He's nigh eighteen, ain't he?"

"Yeah. Ain't they always leaving? Good riddance, I say." Jude didn't sound concerned, about Jesse or about who'd do the work around the place.

Grandma had come from the kitchen and heard the last words. She said, "They're always leaving, is right."

"I'm staying, Grandma," I told her. She looked at me and I repeated, "I'm staying."

The Smell of Death

A COUPLE OF weeks after PeeDee went home, Grandma decided we'd go down the mountain and across the highway and through a couple of pastures to visit old Mrs. Norris. She and Grandma had grown up together and now Mrs. Norris stayed by herself in a tiny cabin without even a road into it. I might have been moping around feeling lonesome, so Grandma decided to make the three-mile trek there and back. But the visit wasn't the most exciting part of the day. In fact, we never even got there.

We expected to visit with Annie on our way down the mountain. Before we rounded the last curve to her house, we both smelled something fleshy rotten. A whiff would come through the still air and then be gone. Then I saw them.

"Look, Grandma!" I pointed to the sky over the hill above Annie's house. Great black birds were circling, wheeling, drifting, like they had a wind under them that we couldn't feel.

"Buzzards. Something's dead up there." Grandma paused to spit to the side of the road. "That's what we've been a-smelling. Something's dead over yonder."

I wondered what it was. "Something bigger than a rabbit or squirrel," Grandma said, as if she could read my wonderings.

"A bear? Reckon it's a bear or a deer?"

Grandma shook her head. "We'll see if Annie knows anything about it."

Annie was wondering the same thing. We drank cold buttermilk to the front porch and watched the black creatures circle and occasionally drift to the ground. "The young'uns are down at Flo's getting some cloth she's saved for me. When they get back, they'll go see what it is."

"Let's go find out now," I proposed. "Let's go look. It's not far."

"Too far for me, June," Grandma said. "We've got a long way to go to Ida's."

"I'm not about to go up there," Annie declared. "Why, it might not even be dead! And them buzzards may be tearing it apart."

"It's not alive! You can smell it." My curiosity had doubled simply because they wouldn't go look at the attraction of the scavengers. I could tell they were just going to sit there, drinking buttermilk and talking.

I pouted, sitting in the sunshine, picking beggar-lice off my dress tail, watching the buzzards. After about two minutes, I tried again. "Can I go look. It's right up there. I won't go out of sight. You can see me from here."

"Go on, if you want to," Grandma said. "But don't go out of sight. And watch out for snakes."

I crossed the single-track road and slipped under the barbed wire fence, careful not to snag my dress. I picked my way carefully over the pasture, watching for cow patties and for thistles. It was an open area, dotted occasionally with a clump of blackberry briars or a pile of brush. I looked back and waved a couple of times to assure Grandma and Annie I was okay.

The birds numbered at least a dozen, as far as I could tell. They were bigger than I'd thought, bigger and uglier. I moved slower as the smell increased. I hesitated when something moved nearby. I hadn't seen anything, just sensed movement. I stood still. If it was a snake, it wouldn't come toward me. I heard a slight rustle near me. My blood sent goose bumps to my arms. Then I saw it.

Tom, Annie's old cat, was slinking to my left, intent on whatever it was stalking. Maybe it wasn't aiming for any mouse or grasshopper. Maybe the cat was just as curious as I was. Maybe Tom was just keeping me company. I suddenly wanted some company. In another hundred steps or so, over the crest of the rise, I could surely see what the birds were swooping toward. Now I wasn't so sure I wanted to see. Still I walked a few feet further, Tom now slinking on the ground to the right of me, several yards in front.

Suddenly a big black bird sliced downward from the sky. It hadn't been with the drifters. It looked like it was coming straight toward me with a purpose in mind, and I dodged and fell on my knees. It veered to my right and snatched Tom up by the scuff of his neck. Tom let out a squawk that would wake up the dead, a long yowwwww. I could see his kicking feet and stretched belly as the big hawk soared upward. I guess it got about ten feet off the ground before it dropped the cat and circled upward.

Tom landed in a brush pile and got his feet all tangled up in the loose brush, but in a flash he was leaping out of the pile and running toward Annie's. I raced after him. He was squalling all the way. Grandma and Annie saw me flying through the pasture and scooting under the fence and they met me at the road. They thought I'd been bee stung or snake bit. I was so out of breath that for a minute I couldn't tell them that I was okay, but Tom would never be the same.

"Lordy, young'un, you like to scared us to death," Grandma said. She didn't hug me, but she put her hand on my shoulder and steered me back toward Annie's house. Annie was pale, too, and out of breath from rushing across the road.

"I'll put some salve on that knee," she said. I hadn't even noticed that my knee had landed on a thistle but now it stung like crazy.

"That old Tom's probably all the way to Glenville by now," I said. "That hawk just grabbed him right up—"

"I'm glad I didn't see it myself," Annie said. She shuddered a little. She rummaged on a shelf for the Cloverine salve which she rubbed on my reddening knee.

We never did get on to Mrs. Norris' that day. Annie's children came home, and I told them all about the snatching.

We went looking for Tom, but he wasn't anywhere we could see, not even as far back under the house as Nan, the smallest girl, could crawl. Annie sent the boys to see what was attracting the big birds. She made them take a broom with them, "just to fend them off if need be," she told the boys.

Grandma said, "They look green around the gills," as they reappeared.

"It's a little calf," they reported.

"It's little Star!" Nan started crying. "Remember, we saw that old mama cow and Aunt Flo said she'd had little Star! It was just Monday!" she wailed.

Pretty soon we girls were crying and the boys were looking at their feet. Annie looked paler and paler, with all the misery around her. Grandma took charge.

"You boys get your slingshots and get up there and kill them buzzards. Or at least scare them off. Jude and Louise likely aren't back from town. Sue, you tell them boys of theirs to go and bury the little thing."

"You girls stay back here," Annie ordered. "You don't need to go looking at something that ugly."

That same day, the day of the buzzards, not two hours later, I heard about a real murder for the first time.

"I'm just going to stay here a spell," Grandma told me. "You go on down to Louise and Jude's if you want to. They're likely back by now."

Jude and Louise had gone to Glenville for supplies and a new hoe. We met them coming up the road, tired from carrying stuff. It was a big surprise when Louise opened up a bag and handed candy bars to all of us. I got a Baby Ruth.

"Now get on and play," she instructed. Louise looked strained and white. Jude didn't look too steady on his feet. Sue and I went one way, the other kids wandered off in a different direction. I carried my candy bar with care. I intended to savor it, maybe take just a bite a day until it was gone. And Sue wouldn't tear into hers until I did. We didn't want to play and I didn't want to think about little Star.

I looked down the road and saw Flo's husband Ham coming up the mountain. He never ventured up the mountain because he and Jude didn't get along. And Louise was going back to meet him. They were cousins I think. Sue and I hopped up the bank to walk out of sight above the road. They met in the curve. The rhododendron bushes were thick and we could barely see them in the shadows. Without thinking, I tore open my candy bar.

Louise was talking, in a breathy way. I could barely hear. "Murder...they're saying it was murder." Flo's husband shook his head as if he couldn't believe it. I took a sticky bite. If I leaned any farther over, I'd likely tumble right down on them.

"Taxi driver ...Sylva...blood all over." I heard that. And Louise said, "They're saying...done it. They're looking for him." I didn't hear the name.

"It'll be the electric chair then." Flo's husband gripped Louise's arm. "Will you take him in if he comes up here?"

"I don't know, Ham. They said blood was everywhere."

"Ah, God," Ham said. "He's always been dumber than a sled runner." He turned and went back down the road.

I ate the whole Baby Ruth before I realized it.

Sue and I didn't say a word to each other about the conversation we'd heard. She told me about a story in one of her mother's magazines and I told her about the baby snakes and a little about PeeDee. By the time we got back to Annie's, Louise had told her and Grandma. Zander Hadley was being hunted down for killing a taxi driver in Sylva, the county seat. A big posse was out looking for him. That's all they knew. Zander was Louise's half brother. He'd been named after Alexander Hamilton, but everybody called him Zander.

Later as Grandma and I trudged back to the gray house, I was thinking of that candy bar that I'd hardly tasted and of murder, the word and the meaning.

"Will they catch him, you think?" I asked Grandma.

"He's got no more chance than little Star had once the smell of death was on it," she said.

"Well, is he a bad man?"

"Bad is as bad does, June. That's what they'll say. Guess it's the truth." Grandma stopped to rest. She inserted snuff into her mouth with her sassafras brush. "Zander's not done much good in this life, going from one job to another, one woman to another. Trifling. Never settled down."

I thought about what she said. Not settling down was just about the worst thing you could do. Whenever I heard bad things about people, men and women, it always seemed to come back to "they couldn't settle down." I'd heard it about my mama. But murder was worse than not settling down. I thought some more.

"What's the electric chair?"

"Lord, June, don't ask so many tom-fool questions. You've got ears too big for your head, you do. Who said anything about the electric chair?"

My shoulders drooped a little. I didn't want Grandma to quarrel at me. Even if I did miss PeeDee, I really didn't want to go home. Bruton's Mountain was a lot more exciting with its buzzards and hawks and Baby Ruths than staying in our little house with Mama. Mama was especially fretful in the summer. She was always telling me I was underfoot and in her way.

"Don't worry your pretty little head about it," Grandma said. "It's not happened yet. Maybe won't. If Zander done it, he's likely far away by now."

"Reckon he'll go out west?" I cheered up at the thought of Zander, whom I'd never seen, roaming over the plains with the buffaloes and mountain lions. He'd wear high boots and buckskins with a fringed shirt and look just like Wild Bill Hickok.

Grandma smiled faintly. "He's probably half way there already."

Horseshoeing

FLO'S HUSBAND WAS generally considered a worthless man, good for just one thing. He could shoe a horse quicker and smoother than anybody else around. And that counted for something. That was the only work he ever did, and he did that only when he felt like it. Everybody knew he felt more like it if a pint or quart of moonshine passed hands before he made up his mind.

"Don't know if I'll have time to get to him today," Ham would say, likely not even rising from his rocking chair on the front porch.

"Well, I'm needing it done right bad," the man holding the reins would say. "You shore you're busy now?"

"Might be."

Anybody with any sense knew that was the time to reach into the sack thrown across the horse's back or reach into an overalls' pocket and bring out a brown paper bag. Moonshine didn't travel out in the open. A brown paper bag, usually twisted at the top, signaled that it was time to start the negotiations in earnest.

"I'd leave him here if you can get to him today." The bag would be strategically placed in plain view.

"Reckon I've got a little time on my hands, if you're not in a big hurry." Ham would heave himself from the chair. Like his wife, he was big. Flo couldn't fit into the rocking chair, and he scrapped the sides getting up.

Even Grandpa couldn't push Ham any faster than Ham wanted to go. Odd had lost a shoe and had to be shod, and Grandpa was in a hurry. I sat on the porch steps and watched. Flo was making us a pan of fudge. She knew the shoeing would likely get done, especially since Grandpa was known to sip only the best.

After a few exchanges about the weather and the rush job Grandpa had and about how Odd had lost the shoe, Grandpa hauled out the brown bag, Ham hauled his bulk from the chair, and they led the horse around the house to the stocks.

I had mixed feelings about coming down to Flo's with Grandpa, but Grandma was feeling bad and told me to bring her some aspirin from Flo's medicine cabinet. She was confident Grandpa would forget it. I wanted to visit Flo because she was sure to be cooking something sweet and she liked company. But I didn't much like to see the horse shoeing. I rode part of the way down the mountain on Odd, but with his tender foot, I felt better walking behind.

I moved inside and watched out the window as Odd was placed in the stocks. Ham had four poles in the ground with steadying poles lashed and nailed to them.

"Ever see a runaway horse, June?" Flo stirred with great concentration.

"Nope."

"It's about the scariest thing I've ever seen. That and mad dogs just petrify me."

I shivered. Big dogs running loose scared me. I couldn't even imagine a mad dog.

"A panicky horse is a dangerous thing," Flo continued. "Ham is good at gentling any scared thing, but you can't gentle something that's just a-racing through the fields."

Ham was busy at the fire, heating up the horseshoe. Odd was restless, shifting his weight around, but Grandpa didn't look worried. He was seated in the shade of the shed.

Flo went on. "Somehow, that mare that Al down at the general store, you know Al? Well, Al was leading that mare across the road, back to pasture. He'd had her over letting those little tourist girls ride her behind the store, and he started back to the pasture. Some said a bee must've stung her or some boy might'a shot her with a slingshot. But she started a-running like crazy, knocked Al down right in the middle of the road. It's a miracle some truck didn't come along and flatten him, right in that bad curve. That mare went like the wind, right down the road. Some boys took out after her, scared her even more. She got her reins tangled up in them trees down there."

Flo pointed out the door. "By the time she came through here, she was foaming, her eyes as big as saucers. I think she went crazy. She tore up my dahlias and trampled the edge of the corn patch there. She was glistening with sweat and such eyes I've never seen—and never hope to again."

Flo fanned herself and held the wooden spoon up. The fudge was ready to pour on a plate to cool.

The only time I'd ever seen horses, they'd been peacefully grazing in the pasture or they'd been controlled by Johnnie or Grandpa or somebody. I couldn't quite imagine a horse just running around wild like that.

"I'd like to see that," I said.

"Lord, no, you wouldn't, honey," Flo said. "I've had nightmares ever after."

"Nightmares?" I giggled. Flo wiped her shiny face with a dishcloth and laughed a little.

"Nightmares is right!" She set the plate of fudge on the table in front of the window. "It'll be a few minutes before we can eat it," she said. "That mare of Al's was worth a lot of money. Him and some boys followed her as best they could. And Lord, when they finally caught her, she'd run right into a bobwire fence, was cut up around the throat. And she was down in her legs. Al had to send a boy home for his gun. And he had to pay the boys to help him dig a grave on Monroes' property, that's where she ended up, to bury her."

"I'm glad I didn't see it," I said.

"Well, word got around among the tourists. They was at the lake. They took up some money to help Al out. But he's not bought another horse yet. Says he can't sleep either. A runaway horse is a sight you want to miss in this lifetime."

She sighed. I thought about the buzzards circling the little calf and about the horse and about Zander's murdering the taxi driver. It seemed like living was a dangerous thing. We both eyed the fudge and waited.

BETWEEN SUMMERS

My Red Raincoat

RED. MY LITTLE red raincoat. Red and hooded. My new "ready to start to school" coat. I was so proud of it. It almost reached my ankles so I could grow into it. Mama had to plan on me getting bigger, so practically everything new was bought a little too big, but I had my red raincoat, big enough to last for two or three years anyway. I gloried in it. I tried it on dozens of times, admiring its splendid color. I thought that PeeDee would really admire it, and I really hoped for rain on the first day of school.

When I despaired of the rains ever coming that fall, a good one arrived on Sunday night. Monday morning dawned damp and I was ready. I wore one of my flour sack cotton dresses rather than my usual corduroys.

On our way to school, the five kids who lived down the road and I had to pass the terrible bull pasture. It was about midway between our starting out and our arriving at the two-story wooden school building, so I had plenty of time to anticipate my dread, to feel the little stone of fear begin its bulbous growth, fed by the older kids' teasing.

"Oh boy, I wonder if it's in a bad mood today?"

"Let's throw rocks at it. Make it mad."

"Come on, June. Scaredy cat, it's on the other side of the fence. It can't get us."

But it had gone through the fence once and had run Mr. Boyd back to his truck.

This damp, soggy morning, I entreated and was allowed to wear my new red raincoat. I walked proudly into the living room to show off. My face glowed. "How do I look, Daddy?"

Daddy said that I was right pretty in my dress and that the little coat was the handsomest thing this side of Yancey County. I was just ready to preen off, my lunch bucket in hand, when he said, "Now watch out for that bull, honey. Red just sets'em off. You watch out now."

Suddenly I remembered the other times I'd heard red associated with bulls and how they hate it. The fear blossomed full grown, right up into my throat, choking me. Daddy had turned back to his coffee cup, his face in his hands. I had to go down to the road to meet the other kids. Sure enough, we were hardly started when Brenda, in the fourth grade and sometimes my ally and protector, let out a shriek. "Lord, look out for the bull today! That red raincoat will get him going for sure."

I was hoping the rains would suddenly pour down and shrink both the raincoat and me into oblivion. We trudged on. I wanted to throw up, but the fear rooted in my stomach and sprouting against the back of my mouth had almost closed off my breathing. Yet I tagged along, like the runt in a pack of young puppies. If I slowed, they yelled, "Come on, we'll be late. Come on. We can't wait on you all day."

As we rounded the final bend in the road at the big apple tree before the long level stretch along the river that culminated in the bull's pasture, my feet were sluggish but my mind was frantic.

"Oh please, Mr. Tin Truck, please come along and offer us a ride." On occasional mornings, a man whose name we did not know, someone who apparently lived way on up the road, someone who drove a pickup truck with a homemade tin top on it would stop and we would all pile into the back of the truck. We called him simply, "Mr. Tin Truck."

The others picked up speed as we inevitably neared the bull pasture. We passed Mr. Boyd's dairy barn and his house on the left. Stretching far above the house was a vast field, fairly steep. If you cut off from the highway and went straight up the field and then straight down on the other side, you came to a gravel road that joined the highway maybe half a mile beyond the bull pasture. Some afternoons we went that way home although it was much farther; I was always glad to walk the extra mile or so to avoid the bull. Other times the bull was not in its pasture in the afternoon or it was lazing down by the river under the willow trees and was not inclined to be aggravated by four or five school kids.

It was the mornings that were terrible. Then the bull was rested and lively. The bull was not the storybook picture of a prize bull, not particularly broad shouldered or broad rumped. It was kind of scrawny, but it was the only bull I had ever seen and I didn't know that it wouldn't win any contests for best bull features. It was spotted, mud-color spots on dirty cream skin. Its curved horns were not graceful and one tip was broken. It had a ring in its black nose, and its nostrils were always wet. When it flung its head around, moisture, sometimes foamy, sometimes clear was slung from its face to its neck.

At one end of the pasture, the end we approached on our way to school was the gate: a shiny new steel affair that caught the sunlight most mornings and flashed me a warning that I was approaching the dreaded place. In contrast to the fierce bright gate, the fence was merely four strands of barbed wire, rusty and broken in some places. The fence posts were askew and mismatched, some old with gray-green moss and some shored up in some semblance of strength.

Apparently Mr. Boyd never constructed a new fence; he simply added a post or a strand of wire now and then. I knew that if that bull ever wanted to it could knock one of those fence posts down easily enough, and once in a while, in fact, it had. Daddy would come home and report that "Old man Boyd's bull got out. They caught it down near the mill, cornered it next to that high bank." or a neighbor would say on a Saturday morning, "Don't let June go down to Baxters to play today. They hadn't caught Boyd's bull last I heard."

"Come on, June," urged Brenda, taking my cold hand for a moment. "We're going to be late."

"Yeah, come on," yelled Bobby. "I can't wait to see what the bull's gonna do when it sees that raincoat of yours."

For all their bravado, the other kids were surely just a little afraid of the bull. The boys expected, of course, to race up the steep bank on the left side of the road and get up a tree if the bull really broke out. And Brenda, I don't know if she was simply fearless or dumb. She seemed impervious to the boys' laughter and comments, both about the bull and about her budding figure and hips.

The sun glinted on the fence and into my eyes. It brightened the hateful raincoat that slopped around my ankles. Why did the sun have to suddenly lighten the day? Why wasn't the sky raining, sending the bull to the shelter of the willow trees. Why was I wearing a red raincoat? Why not a safe green that would blend into the scrubby bushes along the side of the road? Why had I begged for a red raincoat, red of all things? Why hadn't my mother insisted on the ugly green that she had first pointed out in the store? Why hadn't I known that red was a terrible color, a tempting color, a color made to flaunt at bulls, a color made to infuriate them?

I hung back as the others went on past the bright gate. The bull was there, right up at the fence, its back to us, its tail tossing over its dirty rear. It was facing the way we were headed. It looked around, red eyed with a snort of malice. With a certain glee, and different degrees of speed and deliberation, the others crossed to the other side of the highway.

I couldn't go back home in disgrace although I felt sick enough to never go to school again. I could not march the long march to the other end of the bull pasture in my red raincoat. The bull had not yet spotted me, and already it was tapping the ground with an amazingly delicate movement of its forefoot. The other kids were several feet in front of me and the bull was moving along the fence at the same pace as they.

I saw my salvation. At the bottom of the steep bank was a ditch, and only last week it had been cleaned out by the highway department. So it was slightly deeper than usual when it was snarled with briars, overgrown grass, and the usual assortment of beer bottles and paper debris. I dashed to the ditch and lowered myself carefully. Just crouching wouldn't do it; too much of my red back would surely still show. I left my lunchbox beside the highway. Hunkered down as far as possible I scampered along on all fours, my chest heavy as if a fifty pound bag of chicken feed was bolted to it.

I was almost even with the other kids who had not paid much attention to me, being too occupied with the pawing, now snorting bull. Then Bobby looked for me and yelled, "Come on, June. Show this old bull your red rain coat."

"Hey, where are you? Scaredy cat! scaredy cat!" When they realized that I was the red movement in the muddy ditch they jostled each other and laughed. "Look at her go! A little red boodle bug!"

Let them laugh. I was moving along, my eyes down, partly to avoid sharp rocks or broken bottles in the ditch, partly to let the tears drop directly on the ground. I could tell when I was near the end of the pasture. The steep bank became a rock cliff at the edge of a dangerous curve and the ditch abruptly ended. But the end of the ditch also meant the end of the pasture and my freedom.

I jumped up and onto the pavement, running around Dead Man's Curve "on the inside" as we had been warned never to do because too many drivers lost control of their vehicles in its sharpness.

The others, snorting loudly at the frustrated bull and laughing also with relief disguised as bravery, ran to catch up with me. My hands were muddy, the cuffs and hem of my red raincoat filthy. My knees were scratched and my dress bedraggled. I looked worse than the old granny woman who in her semi-madness hung around Snyder's Store and glared at us in the afternoons.

The rest of the day went by without leaving a memory in my head. That afternoon, in silence and shame and alone, I trudged up the gravel road and up the steep field and down the other side. I wished PeeDee was with me. It was the first time I had walked all the way home by myself. I knew then that some of my journeys would be lonely ones.

My daddy enveloped me in his arms, long before I reached our porch. My mother had gone visiting somewhere. He had started to look for me when the others reported that I was going the long way home. He could tell by their faces that something had happened and had wormed it out of Brenda, who was in a state of adult disfavor for letting me walk alone. My daddy picked me up and carried my muddy self home. He made Bobby go back and get my lunch box.

"I don't care what your mama says," Daddy whispered, "that red raincoat is too big for you. I'm taking you to the store tomorrow to get you a new one. Maybe a pretty yellow one."

PeeDee Gets Hurt

THAT VERY FALL, I thought I'd lost PeeDee for good. I thought she was dead. We were playing softball in early September. Hardin was batting. He was a tall boy, silent as all the Hyatts. And a good ball player. We were lucky to have him on our side, and we were ahead eight to six. Recess was almost over. When the bell sounded we had to quit, so we wanted to get one more home run and really beat the other side. Hardin stepped up to bat, and he hit the ball hard.

He also slung his bat—hard. PeeDee and I were standing five or six feet behind him. The bat caught her square on the forehead and she went down without a sound, just hit the ground. Hardin didn't know what he'd done till he rounded second and saw us clustered around PeeDee. He kept coming and touched home plate. Meanwhile, somebody ran to get the teachers and Mr. Clontz.

I couldn't stand the sight of PeeDee, unconscious, maybe dead. I was afraid to touch her and the big girls kept saying, "Stand back. Don't smother her."

I squatted next to her foot and touched it, just keeping myself calm. Mr. Clontz carried her into his office. He didn't want me to stay but Mrs. Sherrill said, "June's her best friend." PeeDee's forehead had a big pump knot already. Mrs. Sherrill put a wet towel on her head. "She's breathing, June. Don't worry."

It took a long time for Dr. Garret to get there, and before he did, PeeDee opened her eyes and said, "Ouch. My head hurts." Those were blessed words to my ears.

There was just a little blood, a thin line. The bat had hit solid. PeeDee got her forehead washed in alcohol or something, not even a bandage. The doctor said the air would do it more good. "You're not going to feel good for a few days, young lady, but you'll be okay. Stay at home a couple of days. No quick movements. Call me if you get dizzy. You're tough."

"She's tough," I agreed. The doctor looked around. I don't think he'd seen me. Mrs. Sherrill had set me down on a chair and told me to stay out of the way.

I guess somebody went up to the Rednells' house to tell them about the accident. Maybe the doctor told my uncle Cade. He came and took us to my house, saying it'd be okay with PeeDee's parents. She stayed with us the rest of the week.

The Halloween Carnival

A HIGHLIGHT OF the school year was the Halloween Carnival. Each class had one or more special booths. Tubs for bobbing for apples sat ready, and balloons hung in front of the blackboard with numbers of prizes in them. We could "fish" for prizes behind a curtain, walk in the cakewalk to win luscious, heavy cakes, play bingo. We could be blindfolded and led through the scary Haunted Room where furry creatures guided our hands into slick spaghetti and a disguised voice told us we were squishing worms from the grave and all kinds of gruesome things.

And there were raffle tickets and door prizes. I was a sucker for expecting to win. Mama snapped at me: "Everybody can't win, June. Spend your dollar on something sure." But every year I hoped, and so far Mama had been right. Two or three times I'd circled the table displaying the prizes, admiring a special one.

I couldn't believe my ears when Mr. Clontz called out yet another winning number—mine this time! People had been winning all kinds of things that merchants in Sylva had donated: a box of chocolate covered cherries, towel sets, a set of kitchen knives. I had my heart set on the giant jigsaw puzzle showing a picture of Washington DC. I was pretty sure nobody had claimed it. When I went up to the front of the room, with Daddy right behind me, the principal handed half my prize to me, the other to Daddy: two quarts of motor oil, Quaker State. I tried to smile. I stepped back out of the limelight and bit my lip. We didn't even have a car. The motor oil was heavy and awkward. I handed it to Daddy.

"Don't look so disappointed, June. Winning anything is better than nothing."

"No, it's not. I wanted that big puzzle." I loved jigsaw puzzles. I saw that Mrs. Kincaid was carrying it toward the door. I'd spent eight of my dollar's worth of dimes Daddy had given me on the raffle tickets. Still I rummaged in my pocket hoping I'd overlooked one. If I had I was going to go back through the Haunted Room just so I could forget my troubles and squish my fingers in worms from the grave.

I headed toward the door. The drawing signaled the end of the Carnival anyway, and Aunt Mattie and Uncle Cade were giving us a ride home.

Daddy stood outside, smoking a cigarette. "Ready to go, June? Your mama's just coming."

"I'm ready," I mumbled. "Where's that old motor oil?"

"Now what would we need with that, June? I traded it for something."

He put into my hands the big puzzle. The overhead light illuminated the Washington Monument.

Naming Names

"JUNE LEE, THAT'S a right pretty name," PeeDee said. We sat in the early April sunshine, cracking walnuts. They were dried out and shriveled, but it was something to do. We rubbed the walnuts in a little pile of salt between us before plopping them into our mouths.

She grinned. "But it's a mighty wonder they didn't name you July, being born when you was, there in the middle of the month."

"Well, Mama said she expected me in June and she'd decided on my name if I was a girl. Mama's not likely to change her mind once it's made up."

When I'd asked them about my name, Daddy had tried teasing Mama.

"Guess she miscounted her numbers," he said. Mama blazed out at him, "You should talk, Carl Bruton. You can't count worth a diddly squat." Daddy winked at me, but he shut up and went back to sharpening his knife.

"I like your name, too," I told PeeDee. "Prudence Delilah has a real stylish sound to it. Names are funny things. Sometimes they fit and sometimes they don't."

"Same as places," she grinned. I had turned beet-red at school that day. The teacher had been doing geography and I wasn't paying much attention until I heard the word "Canada." I perked up and listened while she described the wheat fields, the Yukon (that I knew about from the radio), polar bears, and terrible blizzards. I'd blurted out, right out loud, "My daddy's working in Canada right now."

Mrs. Sherrill stopped writing on the board and frowned at me. A little titter went around the room. "Are you sure about that, June?" Her voice was kind. It always was, but she didn't believe me.

"Yes, I am," I asserted. "He's over there right now."

Everybody looked at me. A boy spoke up. "She means over toward Cullowhee," he said. "Canadee."

Mrs. Sherrill unfrowned her face. "Oh yes," she said, "I'd forgotten about that little community. It's not the same place, June. Your dad's working just a few miles from here. The Canada I'm talking about is close to a thousand miles from here." I wanted to slip under my desk, but PeeDee tugged on my pigtail from the desk behind me. That sharp pain made me sit straight again. I didn't say a word the rest of the day.

"Still seems dumb to me," PeeDee said now, "to name that little old place for a big country like Canada. I guess somebody went up there and when he come back he just dropped the name on that store and church."

I thought about names. "Yeah, like who would ever think that the principal's name was Ralston. Rawws ston. Mr. Clontz with a name like that." We giggled.

"And imagine naming a baby Tullulah!" We knew there was a place named Tullulah Gorge in Georgia, but one day we'd been told about the famous singer. The name struck us both as funny. Mrs. Sherrill almost made us leave the assembly.

June seemed dull as dishwater compared to my friend's name. She preferred PeeDee to her full name. She said her mother wanted to call her Prudence and her daddy wanted to call her just plain Mary. Her mother told the doctor who'd come to the house in time for the cleaning up after the delivery, "Set down Prudence on the certificate." Her father exploded and shouted she was just another Delilah. He'd been drinking heavily all day. The doctor put down Delilah after Prudence—and that's what she was officially.

Of course, any boy who called her that could expect pretty soon to be sporting a bloody nose. If the culprit was too big or too old for PeeDee to bruise, she found some way to get back at him.

One day Ben Amos made the mistake of yelling "Prudence Delilah" at her across the playground. She stuck out her tongue at him, a weakling response. Then we went to the cafeteria for lunch. We sat at long tables on benches worn smooth by much sliding along them. When Ben tried to stand up to reach for some salt, he fell right into a plate of wieners and beans. His shoelaces had been tied together. I didn't see PeeDee do it and that's what I told the teacher on duty, but she kept both of us in during recess.

As if I could have stopped PeeDee even if I'd wanted to. Like she said later, "What's a little less recess compared to the look on Ben Amos's face!" When everybody laughed and hooted, Ben was a pretty good sport about it. He grinned and started curling his tongue around his lips to slurp up a bean or two. I liked Ben better after that. He could have caused trouble for us. He didn't and he called her PeeDee after that.

Witlings Defame Her

SCHOOL ITSELF WAS an adventure for me. There was always something happening, and I learned new words. I liked gathering in the auditorium every morning to pledge allegiance to the flag and to sing "America the Beautiful" and "The Old North State Forever." We sang with gusto even if we didn't know what we were singing.

"What's a witling?" I asked Mrs. Sherrill one day, after we'd belted out our North Carolina state song with its line: "Though scorners may sneer at and witlings defame her, still my heart swells with gladness whenever we name her." The only thing I thought of when we sang was something like a beaver or an otter, neither of which I'd ever seen.

She smiled. "In the eighteenth century, Alexander Pope...let me see, June. Hmm. I guess you could say a witling's a dim-witted smart alec." That ruined my theory about otters and beavers, but I called Ben Amos a witling the first chance I got when he was teasing Brenda. I could tell he didn't know what I'd called him and he wasn't about to ask.

Soon after that, during our Friday before Easter picnic, the woods near the white two-story frame schoolhouse caught on fire. We had returned to the building for one last class after a big lunch outdoors. The fire truck from nearby Sylva roared onto the school ground. We were "evacuated" (a big word I stored away for future use). The teachers rang the big bell, lined us up, and marched us back out onto the playground, just like our practice fire drills. Maybe the school was in danger, but I bet they just wanted to see what was happening too. We all stood at the edge of the school ground, opposite the wooded area where the fire smoldered.

We learned some Abad words" from the firefighters, though, as they struggled with a long hose. PeeDee and I elbowed each other and rolled our eyes. The rumor spread right through our ranks that some of the big boys, had started the fire when they sneaked into the woods to smoke.

"Uh Oh," PeeDee said, "Ben Amos and Lester's going get it now."

"How do you know it's them?"

"Everybody knows they smoke." PeeDee always knew more than I did about worldly things. Seems like half what I know she told me.

After we were herded back in, the big boys got punished. Not for setting the fire. Nobody confessed and nobody could prove who'd been in the woods. Ben had smarted off to the principal and Lester had backed him up. Nobody smarted off to Mr. Clontz and got away with it.

Mr. Clontz called the boys to the front of the room. Ben bent over the desk and Mr. Clontz swung the paddle. It clanked against the Prince Albert can in Ben's back overall pocket. We all kept our faces serious. Mr. Clontz's neck turned red and he swung four more times, clanking each time. He wasn't going to ask the boy to remove the tobacco can. When Lester bent over, though, Mr. Clontz took the Prince Albert can from his back pocket. Lester set his face firm as cement and kept his eyes open. But Ben got the worst of it. For days, the boys teased him about the print of a prince on his backside. I always thought of him when we sang "The Old North State."

Another New Word

MARY LOU STOOD on her toes at the stone water fountain and let the perpetual upward spout of water flow into the thin no-color balloon. She was intent on her task and I was intent on watching her. We didn't hear Mr. Clontz approach. And we weren't prepared for the shock in his voice.

"What have you girls got there?"

Mary Lou jumped and dropped the no-color balloon in the fountain's basin.

"Nothing," I said. Mary Lou wiped her hands on her dress.

Mr. Clontz's face was red, and he gave Mary Lou a sort of pat on the backside to dislodge her from the fountain's stepping stone. She stood back and we watched him pick up the flimsy piece of rubber, now empty of water. He held it with distaste between thumb and forefinger and looked from side to side. There wasn't a trash can anywhere nearby.

Where'd you get this?" His questions seemed way out of line for our harmless activity. This time Mary Lou answered.

"Over in the woods yonder. We was just playing up there." She was ready to cry at another demanding question. I saw PeeDee coming to join us.

"What's wrong with that?" I asked. "It's not off limits." I pointed to the very edge of the playground. The actual woods were "off limits" but there was a section of bushes and more or less cleared area where sometimes the older boys went to tell dirty jokes and sometimes we girls went just to keep the boys from hogging the place.

"My God. What next?" It didn't seem like an appropriate response from the principal who still held the wet object. Mr. Clontz was a nice man and our school was his first principalship. It seemed sometimes that every incident opened new worlds for him, but I didn't see any reason for his dismayed look this time.

PeeDee kind of smirked at the principal's dilemma. Then with a certain presence of mind she took from her pocket her

61

lunch bag. Her mama made her bring the bag home so it could be re-used until it became limp with creases and stained. She handed the bag to Mr. Clontz who took it with evident relief and tucked the no-color balloon in it, crumpled it up, and then put it in his pocket.

He didn't exactly meet PeeDee's eyes as he said, "Thank you. This will do."

He walked off, muttering something to himself about having a teachers' meeting later that day.

"What's he upset about?" I asked.

"Why'd he take it?" Mary Lou wanted to know. "It was mine. I found it."

PeeDee looked around. No other students had come to the fountain. Recess was over and we should be back in the building. She lowered her voice anyway.

"Don't you know nothing? Don't you know what that was?"

Mary Lou and I shook our heads. Something to fill up with water is all I could tell.

"That was a thing that boys use to put over their, you know, their things."

"What things? That ain't going to cover nothing." I thought PeeDee had decided to tease Mary Lou, and I didn't like it. "Little old piece of rubber or something."

"It's to put on their peters when they don't want to make babies," she said. Even PeeDee, whom practically nothing bothered, was looking furtive and just a little embarrassed.

"Their peters!" Mary Lou and I exclaimed the words exactly together.

"That's too big for my brother's little old thing," Mary Lou declared. She made a circle with her thumb and finger to show the size of the ring around the object.

"Well, I don't know how that'd keep from making babies," I said.

"It keeps the stuff in that squirts out, when they do it."

"What stuff?" I couldn't get her sentence straightened out. Mary Lou tried to look worldly. I was at a disadvantage, not having any brothers, I guess.

"The baby stuff, silly." Mary Lou definitely looked superior now. "It's real sticky. Mama was fussing at Charlie about it and I heard her." But she looked puzzled. "It must leak out at night. Charlie ain't about to have no baby. He's not even got a girlfriend."

Mrs. Sherrill came out the door and saw us. "You girls get in here this very minute. Recess has been over and you know it." She didn't sound prepared to listen to any excuses, and I didn't think this subject was something I'd ask about.

"Yes, ma'am. We're coming."

For awhile that afternoon, I pondered on the new knowledge I had, but clearly I didn't know enough. I couldn't quite connect up the animals I'd seen doing it with the human beings in my life. Not in any way that made sense of the balloon Mr. Clontz was upset about. I thought about it while we were doing long division and I decided to ask the principal.

"Mr. Clontz." I caught up with him after school, just as he was about to open his office door. "Can I ask you something?"

"Huh, sure, June. What can I do for you?"

"What was that water balloon you took away from Mary Lou?"

He stood there for what seemed like a long time. I got impatient. PeeDee had rushed out ahead of me and she'd be waiting for us to walk home. I thought he wasn't going to answer me.

"It's called a prophylactic, June. But that's a word you shouldn't go around saying. Nice girls don't know—don't talk about them. You'll find out when you're grown up. And you're a long way from that." He rumpled up the hair on the top of my head. "Now, don't go saying I told you and don't ask me any more questions." He grinned as if we were spies together. "Not unless you want me to lose my job over a word."

"Well, what's it for?" I felt brave, talking to the principal all by myself.

"Well, it's to keep a boy's sperm from, from escaping. Now June, get out of here. This conversation's closed."

I raced out of the dark hall with its oily floor. PeeDee was waiting on the steps. "I guess I know more than you do!" I couldn't help it. I'd just learned a new word, two new words.

"What do you mean?" PeeDee said.

"That—that thing," I'd lost the first word already. "That's to keep the squerms in"

"Squerms?" She giggled. "Sperm is the word. Sperm, squerm, germ."

I giggled too. "I'll race you to the bridge!" We ran off. As we walked along, I told her I couldn't tell anybody else and she couldn't either or Mr. Clontz might get in trouble. Every few minutes we'd look at each other and burst into giggles and chant our new chant: sperm, squerm, germ, sperm, squerm, germ.

At the next assembly, Mr. Clontz announced that the area where Mary Lou had found the whatyoumaycallit was off limits. A few older boys who smoked groaned and Mrs. Sherrill cleared her throat. PeeDee whispered, "Guess there's some sperm squerms loose out there." We just about choked on our giggles.

Selling the Grit

THAT SPRING WHEN I was going on nine I begged and begged and finally was allowed to sell *The Grit*. It was a weekly paper from somewhere out west that Daddy sometimes brought home with him. It had stories and recipes and all kinds of advertisements.

My week's supply was delivered every Friday to the slanted locust post with our rusty mailbox on it. The packet was too big for the box, but I grabbed it and carried it up the dirt road to our house. In late May a few tourists were down at Baxter's Tourist Cabins on the river.

In my short three weeks in this new money-making enterprise (following saving Blue Horse coupons and selling Cloverine Salve), I had sold the ten papers only to Daddy, Aunt Mattie and Uncle Cade, one of Daddy's friends who worked in the woods logging with him, old Mrs. Hall two miles across the cove, Mr. Freeman down at the store, and one teacher at school. I could tell I was not making much money this way. I figured I could count on the tourists who went in and out of the cabins during spring and summer. Ben had even promised to take over for me when I went to stay with Grandma and Grandpa. I wanted to really make some money, sixty or seventy cents a week maybe.

I kept on at Mama until she said, "Go on then. Don't bother me. And hurry right back."

As I rushed off, newspaper bag on my shoulder, already cutting the flesh through my overalls, she called again, "And don't you go in any cabin."

The three or four adults looked up as I approached. "What can we do for you, little lady?"

"I'm selling newspapers. Want to buy one?" I twisted my pigtail and looked brave.

"What kind of paper?" A man tossed me a quarter. "Keep the change, kid."

"We didn't come here to read." One man kept cleaning his fishing pole.

I pocketed the quarter and handed over a paper, saying, "*The Grit.*"

He looked at the paper and tossed it onto the picnic table.

"That's not the paper," he said, but he looked at me with a look I had not seen before.

The woman picked up *The Grit* and said something under her breath. I didn't understand, but I knew her words weren't complimentary. They all looked at me. It hit me not quick but heavy. They felt sorry for me.

Daddy had that look when he had to shoot Buttercup, the little calf that didn't make it out of her mother right. And Mrs. Sherrill looked that way at Yvonne when they came to school to get her when her mother was so sick. The look stuck my bare feet to the ground and I couldn't move. The tourists went back to messing with their fishing equipment.

The news bag was awfully heavy. It weighed a ton, but I lifted my brown eyes and said, "Thank you, Mister."

Then I ran like crazy back home where *The Grit* was the paper.

SELLING *THE GRIT* was not as much fun as I had hoped. I didn't ever stop at the tourist cabins again, but there were other obstacles, four-legged ones.

"I don't want to go today," I pouted.

"You've got a job to do," Daddy said, his voice edged with sympathy. "You got the money to send them back?"

He indicated the bundle of papers in their canvas bag. So I picked them up, gravely chose one and handed it to Daddy. He dug into his pocket and put a dime in my hand.

"That's one," he said.

I walked down the steps, waving a little goodbye as Daddy watched from the porch. He didn't know I was deathly afraid of meeting mean old dogs. Seems like almost every house had one or two that didn't want anybody coming near the front porch. Last week I'd nearly passed out before Tommy Sutton rushed out to yell at his long-legged spotted hound. I hadn't told anybody but my best friend about the dogs.

"My bones just melted, PeeDee," I'd told her. "But I was stuck there, stone still. I couldn't move."

PeeDee grinned just a smidgen. "I'm imagining a melted statue," she said. "A big stone melting away." I had to grin back at her. It helped at that moment, but now I wasn't so sure.

As I walked in the deeply rutted road toward the highway, I tried to keep from thinking about the dogs so I thought about the road. I imagined the dark woods advancing, sending out their vines to entrap, their weeds to spy, like enemies. The stumps and rotting trunks along the side were sentinels, the pretty wild flowers like troops at ease, dotting the way. I made my way like a soldier not sure of where friend left off and enemy lines began. That occupied me until I reached the highway. My first customer's house would be the Suttons. The road broadened near the mailboxes, and I pretended I had safely reached my army's side.

There sat PeeDee, with her feet swinging over the culvert, slashing with a stick at a few weeds.

"Hey," she said.

"What you doing? How'd you get here this early?" I squatted beside her. She was a good two or three miles from home.

"Caught a ride," she said. "I figured I'd go with you today. Not got much else to do."

I didn't believe that. Her mama kept her plenty busy at home. She'd sneaked off and would pay for it later if her daddy found out.

"Let's go," she said, "before the sun's any hotter."

She carried the stick with her. We walked down the highway and turned up at Pounding Mill Branch. I slowed down, paying attention to every dusty little bug and butterfly along the side of the road.

Sure enough, the old dog was sleeping and the minute we saw it, it raised its head and started howling. It raced toward us, rousing two smaller dogs that joined in barking like crazy.

"Now slow down," PeeDee said. She was a few steps ahead. I had stopped dead still. "Come on," she told me, without looking back.

"We'll walk real slow." She kept moving.

The dog was within two feet of us, its hackles raised, its teeth bared. It growled. A big gray tick stuck on its left ear. PeeDee didn't walk right at it. She veered just a little to the side and I was right next to her. She had not raised the stick. The dog was planted firm as a fireplace, its eyes blazing. Still it didn't jump on us. The other dogs hung back just a little. We walked slower than molasses in December. When we were even with the dog, it shifted and growled again. Its gums were black and its teeth had a yellowish-green shine to them.

"Just keep going," PeeDee said.

"What if it comes on us from behind?" I clutched the *Grit* bag. I could swing it one good time, I thought.

"Don't usually do that, dogs don't."

All the way to the yard, that dog stayed even with us, never lowering its hackles. But it didn't come closer than a foot. PeeDee was between it and me, or I could have felt its breath.

"Mr. Sutton," I squeaked. I tried again. "Mr. Sutton, Mrs. Sutton, I got your *Grit* here."

When the screen door opened, old man Sutton, Tommy's grandpa, hobbled out, holding on to the door.

"Git back there, Gory," he said. "Git back under that porch." His voice was not loud but the dog closed its mouth, loosened its legs, and lowered its head. When the old man came closer to the edge of the porch, the dog turned and went to its hollowed-out sleeping spot a few feet from the steps.

Mr. Sutton handed me my money and I gave him the paper.

"He'll get used to you, girl," he said. "He'll know you one of these next times."

"Ever bit anybody?" PeeDee asked.

"He has," the old man said.

Going back down the road, PeeDee told me, "Whatever you do, don't ever try to outrun a dog. You wouldn't make it to the next tree anyway."

"Everything in me says to run," I said, "but I'm like stuck butter!"

"Just stop and then go real slow. Don't raise your hand unless you intend to bash one's head in. And try to keep fear out of your eyes."

Not every house had such a fierce dog, but from most danced a feisty little dog or two or a fierce-looking hound.

"Does it always work, PeeDee?" I felt braver once we were back at the road to my house.

"Don't nothing always work." She swished the stick at some dusty weeds. She sounded like she was talking about more than dogs, but I didn't ask. "You know that. Don't nothing always work." She handed me the stick. "That's why you might need this. Remember what Mr. Clontz said in history class the other day?"

"Speak softly and carry a big stick!"

As long as I carried that stick with me I never got dog bit. Not really. But Mrs. Boyd's little bitty Mexican dog nipped me a couple of times just above the ankles.

PeeDee said, "Being it's from a foreign country, I guess it don't know not to attack from behind."

Molly

LATER THAT MONTH, PeeDee and I were waiting in the May sunshine at Flo's for Daddy and Mama to come back down the mountain. Ham had come with a message for Daddy and we'd rushed to the mountain. They hadn't told me why, and then they left us at the bottom.

"They don't tell us anything," I grumbled to Flo after Daddy said, "You two stay here."

Flo offered us two spoons and the cake pan to scrape. "Don't worry your head about it, June."

"Grown up business, I reckon," PeeDee said. While waiting for the cake to bake, we went to play in the front yard. I heard Flo yell, "Young'uns! June, PeeDee, get in the house quick! Get in here right this minute." She came out on the porch, a scared look on her face.

We looked up from where we'd been throwing jackstones on the hard, swept-clean dirt and jumped to our feet. I bent to grab up the jacks. Flo moved faster than I thought she could and yanked me violently by the arm and almost flung me into

69

the house. A bobby pin had come loose and gray some hair escaped into her eyes.

Flo slammed the door and went to the window. We looked out, too. At the edge of the yard was a mangy dog, staggering around. Foam dripped from its mouth. It was going in circles and speeding up.

"Get brother Andrew," Flo said. I ran upstairs where I knew he was sleeping off a hangover. It was mid-afternoon. Maybe twice a year Flo's oldest brother came and stayed two or three days, "recuperating," he called it. He was a good solid citizen in South Carolina, but he went off on a drunk occasionally and he sometimes found his way to her house.

"Get up, Brother Andrew." I shook him. "Get up. Flo wants you downstairs."

He mumbled something about Aget out of here. I'll be a minute." And he waved me out of the room.

"Andrew!" Flo was at the foot of the stairs. "There's a mad dog right out here in the front yard. A mad dog, do you hear me."

When he stumbled into the room, she had the rifle ready and the bullets on the table. My eyes were big. Everybody knew she always hid the rifle when her brother came visiting. Surely she wasn't going to trust him with the rifle.

PeeDee and I were glued to the window. I had never seen a mad dog before, but I'd heard of them. When the grownup sat around and talked, they usually brought up stories of mad dogs or runaway horses or "gone coot crazy" roosters.

The dog, yellow and mud-caked and thin, its ribs showing, was racing around a couple of Rose of Sharon bushes, closer to the house. So close I could see its eyes and I could also tell it was a mama dog. I can't describe the look in the amber-yellow eyes, like a confused frenzy. Maybe it wasn't seeing anything.

Andrew fumbled with the rifle and Flo was at his elbow. She was wringing her hands and cracking her knuckles and saying under her breath, "Oh god. Oh god. I wish Ham was here. I wish Ham was here."

Ham was a crack rifle shot. Andrew might be good too, but I'd never seen a gun in his hands. Grandma said when he was at Flo's house, the rifle was hidden, back under a bed.

"You've only got one shot," Flo said. I don't know why she said that. She'd laid out three bullets on the table.

"I can hit that there dog at fifty paces," Andrew said. He seemed wide awake now. Gray tufts of hair stood straight out from above his ears, and his forehead gleamed with sweat. "Shame, though. Ain't that old man Aiken's bitch? See that bite out of her ear. That's Molly."

"Shoot her. Shoot her!" Flo's voice was shrill. "She's plumb mad. Any fool can see that."

"Yep." Andrew agreed. "A shame though." He went to the doorway which Flo had opened a bare crack. He held the rifle steady against the doorframe.

I knew the moment he pulled the trigger. I was looking straight into Molly's eyes and she was looking straight back at me, confused and all. I could see in the brownish yellow eyes with flecks of foam around them some sort of question. Andrew's shot was true. Molly jerked high off the ground, not even a yelp, and fell straight down in the dust. Her hind legs twitched just a second or two, but it seemed forever.

Andrew handed the rifle to Flo and held on to the doorframe. "Damn. I need a drink."

"There's not a drop in the house," Flo said. "And now, the cake's burning."

THE SECOND SUMMER ON BRUTON'S MOUNTAIN

Looking for Ginseng

I KNEW GRANDPA was a Republican; I knew he was a Baptist; I knew he went out logging most days. I didn't know he was also a maker of moonshine, a bootlegger. Finding it out almost got me and PeeDee killed.

During my second summer at Grandma and Grandpa Brutons, PeeDee stayed with us almost three full weeks. We picked blackberries and found a mulberry tree high up on the mountain. We looked and looked for Little Beth's grave but we didn't find it. We batted tin cans to each other and honed our softball skills. We tried to ride Oscar, but he put his ears back and brayed "no."

"Let's go hunt ginseng," I said one morning. I wanted more than anything to find two things in life: a sand dollar and ginseng root.

Mama had a snow white sand dollar, a souvenir of her trip to Myrtle Beach. She kept it wrapped in a handkerchief in her dresser drawer. It had crumbled a little around the edges, but when she held it I knew it was special. I asked her about it one time when I'd watched her unwrap it.

"It's a memory, June," she said. "You leave it alone." She let me hold it a second, but afterwards she never looked at it when I was around. A sand dollar represented always sunny faraway places, places with waves and seagulls, places that created memories. I couldn't hope to find one anytime soon.

Ginseng, though, seemed a possibility. It grew on other mountains. Why not on Bruton's Mountain? People talked about how much 'sang sold for and who had dug and sold it, but they were tight mouthed about where they found it. It grew deep in the mountains, in shady, moist, and cool places. I'd never seen it but I'd heard it described often enough. We'd look for plants with three leaves and a clump of red berries.

We should have known something awful would happen after I told two lies in a row. We'd filled up that morning on oatmeal with butter and heavy cream along with two fried eggs each. Still I announced, "Grandma, we're hungry."

"Put some sausage in a biscuit." She didn't look up from her ironing. "The men won't be home to eat today. Take two if you want them."

I quickly assembled four biscuits with sausage. On the back porch, PeeDee found a paper sack for us to put them in, greasy as they were.

"Can we go play at Annie's? She told us to come any day."

Grandma nodded. "Be back by supper time, though. And be good."

So off we went.

In three minutes we were down the road, out of sight of the house. Then we cut off at the branch, heading up the mountain. We reckoned we couldn't get lost if we followed that stream. The undergrowth was thick so we got ourselves sticks to push the brambles out of the way, and we walked right along the bank, sometimes on rocks in the water. The moss along the bank was cool and green. We ventured to either side of the creek to look for the elusive ginseng with its distinctive leaves, but we weren't having any luck. We saw a few tadpoles and a crawdad hole or two. As the creek dwindled, we stuck closer to its banks. We'd grown up on bear stories and panther stories and wild hog stories. Two or three hours later, the creek had become our security. We puffed our way on up the mountain and finally collapsed in a tiny clearing at a bend in the stream.

We pulled out the biscuits and devoured them, cupping our hands in the water to drink. PeeDee put the brown bag in her pocket. We'd just about given up looking hard for ginseng plants, but the laurel and rhododendron thickets were pretty. We picked some flowers and floated them in the shallow creek. It didn't do to rest too long, at least not for me. I was getting uneasy. The woods were quiet.

"I don't even hear a bird," I whispered. When we were walking we talked in a normal tone, but the silence surrounded us and we joined it.

"Maybe they sleep in the daytime," PeeDee said. "It must be twelve o'clock. Can't really tell." The sun was up there, I knew, because it sprinkled dots and slivers around, but not much could get through the trees.

"Look," I pointed to a huge downed tree a few feet away. "That's what Miss Johnson called a 'nurse tree,' remember. 'Cause little trees get nurtured there."

PeeDee nodded. "That was right interesting, what she said. Like trees are like mothers or something. Wonder if they know their children?" That's what I liked about PeeDee. She could say the very thing I was thinking and it didn't seem silly.

We looked at the little trees growing from the dark, mossy tree trunk. I thought about Mama and Daddy and how lonely Mama seemed. PeeDee's family was more like all those little seedlings, at least there were a lot of them. PeeDee didn't talk about her family and I had never been to her house.

I thought she must have fun with all those brothers and sisters for company. She didn't tell me about their fun because she didn't want me to feel bad, being, as I was, "an only child." If I asked her, really wanting to know, "How's your family?" she'd shrug and say, "Okay, I guess. Everything's fine." That was all. So I figured she didn't want me to know what I was missing. When a blue jay squawked nearby, we both jumped.

"Let's go a little farther," I said.

"First one to see a lizard, then we'll turn around." PeeDee and I spent a lot of time aiming for something, first one to hear a screech owl, first one to see a rabbit, first one to spot Old Maybelle coming home to be milked, first one to find a ladyslipper or a jack-in-the-pulpit. We trudged on up the creek, now more like a trickle, maybe a foot or so wide, mostly mud with a tiny sluice of water running through it. I hoped I'd see a lizard pretty soon. I was getting jumpy.

Some un-woodsy sound drifted around my consciousness. I couldn't quite place it. We were standing, heads down, hands on our knees, having just climbed a steep incline rather than follow the stream, just because we wanted to claw our way up holding on to the intricate roots jutting out. We didn't intend to lose sight of the creek to our right.

"Shhhh," I mouthed to PeeDee. It was Johnnie's inside-his-mouth whistle. Johnnie could whistle like any boy, but when he wasn't really thinking of whistling, he made a kind of whistling sound with his tongue and his front teeth without moving his lips. He did it when he was preoccupied, doing chores like cleaning mud off his boots or rubbing down Odd and Even.

PeeDee's eyes widened. She recognized it too. Instinctively we stood still rather than blundering on up the mountain or yelling for Johnnie. The sound told us he was on the other side of the creek and farther up. In the stillness, I heard another sound. Lash, Johnnie's dog. Johnnie was awfully proud of Lash's ability to detect danger. Lash wasn't your ordinary hound. Grandpa had plenty of hunting dogs that he kept mean and hungry and away from the house. Lash was a mixed breed, some said a cross between a shepherd and a collie but smaller than either. Johnnie said he could tell a stranger's scent half a mile away.

"And he can tell me when danger's afoot," Johnnie said.

"Prove it," I'd challenged.

"Can't 'less there's danger lurking," Johnnie said. "Them hackles'll rise up and warn me if a stranger's around."

So I recognized the whimpering of Lash. The same kind of sound that Johnnie's inside-the-mouth whistling made.

PeeDee moved in front of me and motioned for me to follow. Luckily the ground was damp and soggy from a recent rain. Our bare feet made no sound. The paper bag crackled a little in PeeDee's pocket. She stopped and took it out, letting it glide to the ground. She led me up and to the right so we were almost directly across from the sounds. Johnnie was supposed to be with Grandpa logging over on Stevens' Branch Road. I wondered if he had slipped away to meet a girl or something. He usually stayed close by Grandpa's side. We settled behind a large rock outcropping. Now I heard other sounds, sort of like somebody working in the kitchen.

We couldn't see anything, so we eased around to the other side of the rock and squinted through the trees. I heard the sound of glass hitting metal or glass, a clink-clink. Then I saw it. Johnnie was working a still! Grandpa's form came into view. I couldn't see his face because of the trees, but it was a big man dressed in black. PeeDee and I looked at each other. Our mouths were O's.

I'd never seen a still but I'd seen a picture in the Sylva paper one time. I knew it was like a factory for white lightning.

Now here was a still right before our eyes. And Grandpa and Johnnie working it. My stomach felt like a feather pillow being pounded. I knew two things right off: This was a big secret and we better not get caught knowing it.

I was so busy staring at the contraption of buckets and coils that I didn't see the spider on PeeDee's arm for a moment. It must have dropped off the rock onto her bare arm. PeeDee was the bravest person in the world—except about one thing. She had a mortal fear of spiders. If she realized that brown creature was on her bare arm, she'd scream without a thought of the consequences. In an instant I slapped her arm and squished that spider. PeeDee jerked around but didn't utter a sound. I brushed the spider off before she could even see it. But the slap had been heard.

"Somebody's out there," I heard Grandpa growl. His voice told me it was him for sure. Lash whimpered a little at

Grandpa's voice, but his hackles didn't rise. Johnnie had been bent over some jars. He straightened up, checked his dog, and turned around slowly in a circle. We knew we couldn't be seen behind the rock. I prayed there weren't any more spiders ready to fall on us.

"Don't see nothing," Johnnie said. He moved quickly and had a rifle in his hand. He kept checking Lash. Lash's ears were up but that was all. Grandpa spit and wiped his hand across his face. He stepped to the side and when he came back in view he had his pistol, pointing in our direction, up at a forty-five degree angle. His eyes probed the trees. I thought they could almost bore through that rock. Both he and Johnnie kept their feet firmly planted but turned their heads in slow circles, seeming to stare longer in our direction.

"I heard something," Grandpa said again. He too checked Lash for a reaction. "Damn dog."

Johnnie immediately dropped to one knee to stroke Lash's head. Just the week before, Lash had come limping in home and PeeDee and I had carefully inspected his foot and removed a big thorn. Lash mostly ignored us—and everybody except Johnnie,but he had let us ease the thorn out and dab the place with sudsy water.

We crouched behind that rock for a long time. Grandpa and Johnnie went back to work, but Grandpa kept his pistol tucked in his belt. Finally, we looked at each other and without a word began to crawl back the way we had come. We were doing okay until we came to the descent over the roots of the tree. I slipped and slid down the last two feet, making hardly any noise. But it must have been enough. A shot zinged through the air. We panicked and started to run. Another shot whizzed by. We scrambled behind the nurse tree and heard a thunk as a bullet buried itself in the rotting mass, spraying its dark interior.

We lay perfectly still forever. I think I heard Johnnie yell that nobody was around. There weren't any more shots. I marveled at how quiet the woods could be. Where were the squirrels and birds. When a reddish brown lizard rustled across the tree's moss, we both jumped. After a few minutes longer, I mouthed, "Let's go," and PeeDee nodded. We got to the road finally, and in the creek we stopped and washed the mud from our hands and knees. We giggled as we sat in the late afternoon sun drying our feet after swooshing them in the water.

"I peed in my pants," I confessed.

"Me too," PeeDee said. I think she said that to keep me company. We didn't say much as we walked on to the house. I was trying to take it all in. I wondered if Grandma knew. Or Daddy and Mama. They must have, but they didn't talk about it. Come to think of it, they didn't talk about much.

"We'll have some explaining to do," PeeDee cautioned as we neared the kitchen. But Grandma was busy at the stove and hardly glanced at us when we came in. I told her we'd played with Annie's kids all day, and we stayed out of sight till our dresses were dryer and we brushed the dirt from them. We even re-plaited our pigtails.

Grandpa and Johnnie didn't seem a bit different that night. PeeDee and I made sure we didn't stare at them or say a word. We ate our creamed corn and green beans and new boiled potatoes in a silence almost as complete as in the woods. Grandpa didn't like talking at the table. Lots of times we'd go through an entire meal without a word except "pass the salt" or "hand me the cornbread."

PeeDee and I washed the dishes and carried in wood and swept the floor and pretty soon after dark we went to bed. As I went out the back door to the outhouse that night, Johnnie was coming back in. He didn't look at me or say a word. As I went by him, in the glow of the lantern, I saw that he had laid on the back porch a greasy brown paper bag.

The Big Sycamore

FLO HAD BEEN taken to the hospital in Sylva with "her sugar acting up bad" and Grandma and Grandpa went with her, so I knew it was worse than bad. Since Johnnie was over at the Watsons, Grandma left PeeDee and me with Annie and her kids for the night. It was exciting, walking down the road just at dark. Nobody talking much. The shadows moved alongside the road as a slight wind stirred the bushes. I knew they were just shadows and I knew the call of the screech owl and I hoped the rustlings were just rabbits and squirrels getting out of our hurried way. I felt spooky, though, and was glad to see the light, faint and wavering, in Annie's window.

After some cornbread crumbled into glasses of milk, Annie decreed that we should all go to bed. "Nobody's coming back up here tonight," she said. "You young'uns stay quiet now, and don't go waking up the baby."

Pretty soon we were left in the back bedroom, all six of us girls. At first Annie's kids were shy around PeeDee. She was company, after all, more company than I was.

"Let's tell ghost stories," Sue proposed. We all piled onto the bed, ready to be scared.

"I ain't interested in no made-up stories," PeeDee said.

"I know a real story," Sue said in the silence. "I bet they's a dead body over behind the post office, just waiting to be found."

When we finally got the story half-way straight, it turned out that Sue had heard one of her teachers talking to the postmaster's wife who had the day before made a gruesome discovery. In the gulley running behind the small post office, she'd been picking a few raspberries, not paying much attention to anything when she saw a strangely white glare in the dirt. It was a pair of false teeth, in almost perfect condition.

"Just about scared her to death," Sue went on. She went flying in to tell her husband. She wasn't about to touch the things. Even more interesting was that close by they found another plate.

"Mrs. Haliburton said it was a most 'mazing thing," Sue said. "There's bound to be a skeleton in there somewheres." She shuddered dramatically. "It'll likely come out piece by piece." She grabbed her twin sisters by their necks. "And come and get you in the dark of the night!" Beth and Blanche screamed and buried their heads under a pillow. They should have known what Sue would do. She was just purely a storyteller.

We talked about those teeth for awhile. Maybe the false teeth meant a body nearby; maybe somebody just lost them. PeeDee wasn't impressed.

Beth said, "I wouldn't go in that gully for all the world."

"Ah, you won't even go by that old sycamore tree by yourself," Blanche said. "Not even in the daylight. You're a big coward."

"You won't go either," her twin said.

"What big sycamore?" PeeDee asked.

I had heard Annie's kids and Jude and Louise's kids mention the big sycamore, but I'd never heard more than a mention that it was haunted. I knew generally where it was.

"Way down the road, through the apple trees, almost to the highway, they's a big sycamore..."

"And it's for sure hainted," Sue interrupted. "It used to be in a regular forest, way back before the place was cleared for apples and such. Now it's at the edge of the orchard. It's a pretty far piece from here."

"Let's go see it," PeeDee said.

Nobody said a word. We had the kerosene lamp still lit and in its light we all looked pale. I hoped somebody would say something funny and change the subject. Nobody did.

"It's a mighty warm night out," PeeDee said. "We could go see this," she emphasized the next words, "hainted tree."

"In the dark?"

"Moon's coming up," PeeDee said. She went to the window. "It's right clear now." The wind had been rising, though, and I could see clouds that were aiming for the moon.

Nobody said a word.

"June and me'll go then," PeeDee said. "Just give us directions. We'll show you—"

"One time Johnnie put some buckeyes there in broad daylight," Sue said, "and the next day they was gone. That ghost took them. They say it starved to death."

"And now it'll eat anything," Blanche said. "It eats whatever's left for it."

I rubbed my chilly arms. "What kind of ghost is it?" Maybe talking about it would satisfy PeeDee. Maybe she was just showing off.

"It might've been a soldier boy that was hiding in that tree and just died and all the meat fell off his bones. They said it was likely somebody hung hisself but his bones was all over the ground."

Sue paused. "That old tree's been there forever. They said the skull was up in the tree, lodged in a fork, and the rest of the bones was all over the ground."

All the kids were talking at once. Nothing grew just under the tree, where the bones were found, and they'd been found a long time ago. Even now in that semi-circle, nothing grew. And things disappeared from the base of the tree.

Among the local boys, the tree was a "dare spot." Boys were always daring other boys to visit the tree after dark. To prove they'd been there, they left items so they could be checked on the next day. The items were always gone. Of course, now no one left any items of value. Who wanted to risk a good pocket knife or a wallet? But it was a fact that things left at the base did mysteriously disappear. People heard moans and groans from the tree.

"And there's painters close by," Beth whispered. Well, I wouldn't argue with that. I was sure I'd heard the scream of a black panther on Bruton's Mountain. It was a mighty scary sound.

"Painter's not going to come after two of us together," PeeDee said.

I was doomed. She turned from the window. I pulled the sheet from the bed and wrapped it around me twice.

PeeDee took the quilt, a faded yellow and pink double wedding ring pattern and wrapped it around herself. "No point in freezing to death." She rolled her eyes.

"You're not going to go down there! You're not going to leave us here!" The girls yanked the sheet and some baby quilts from the bed and the chest of drawers. Pretty soon we were all wrapped up—on a warm night—and were tiptoeing out the back door. We could hear Annie's light snoring in the other bedroom.

We eased down the hill, through the new cleared ground, making hardly any sound. One of the twins stubbed her toe and made a slight sound, sometimes I'd almost stumble over the edge of the sheet. By some unsaid command, we did not hurry and we did not talk. When we had walked a good half hour, Sue said, "We're getting close."

"Come on up here, then," PeeDee told her. "Lead the way."

"I ain't going in front. No siree."

We approached the giant sycamore tree as a moving wedge. PeeDee in front, me at her heels, Sue and her sisters holding hands, bunched up behind us. The tree was an impressive sight in the moonlight, its trunk knotty and moldy-looking. Suddenly every sound seemed magnified. I could hear myself breathe. We stopped several feet from the tree. Now what would happen? I stared at the tree and could see bleached bones underneath, a skull among the branches. I looked again and couldn't see anything except the tree. And the grassless area underneath. We simply stood there waiting for a sign of some sort. The clouds covered the moon and left us in darkness. Beth or Blanche started to whimper.

"Shut up," her older sister said. Sue was carrying the four-year old Nan by this time.

"Don't let it know we're here," another whispered.

"It can see us in the dark," Sue breathed. We stood stock still and in a moment the moon reappeared. We looked at each other—all still there.

As we looked around, we realized we'd brought nothing to leave at the tree. We couldn't leave the bedclothes and we didn't dare leave our nightgowns. Nobody had a pocket. We had to leave something.

I pointed to Sue's head. As the oldest girl, she'd recently had her hair cut and her straight hair was pulled back on one side, held by a single bobby pin.

"That'll have to do," PeeDee said.

Sue handed over the bobby pin without a word. PeeDee looked at me, and together we approached the tree. She knelt, carefully dusted off a selected spot, and placed the bobby pin at the base of the trunk with a certain amount of ceremony. In the moonlight I saw the sparkle in her eyes and a slight grin.

"Let's show this old tree," she whispered. She held my hand and moved around the tree, reaching for my other hand. Our hands didn't quite meet. The girls didn't come any closer to join us.

PeeDee leaned back and looked at the moon. Slowly she intoned, "We have you now, old tree. Circled under the moon. If you've kept the spirit of the dead one near you, old tree, if you've kept this spirit alive all these years," PeeDee stopped for a moment. I held my breath. I saw her grin, and I knew she was just making up words as she went along, but I didn't know what might happen if you dare to fool with a ghost tree.

"If you've got his spirit, old tree, let it go now!" We were kind of hugging the tree, reaching around it. PeeDee flung our hands free and upward, and at that moment the world went dark. The girls let out little yelps and started running, stumbling over their dragging quilts. PeeDee giggled and I breathed again. Then we took out after the others. We fell a few times in the moments before the clouds again left the moon uncovered. We were back in the bedroom in record time, scrapped and scratched a little and breathing hard.

"Lord a-mercy, what a time!" Sue collapsed on the bed and we all piled in, shedding our quilts and sheets. Everybody started whispering at the same time.

"You young'uns settle down in there," Annie called out, groggy and irritated. "I mean it."

We knew if she came in, we'd have to explain our sweaty faces and dirty feet, so we tried to quieten down. Finally Sue said, "You think it worked, PeeDee? You think that old tree's give up the ghost's spirit?"

PeeDee thought for a minute. "You probably won't ever get your bobby pin back. But I think that ghost's finally on its way home."

We told every ghost story we'd ever heard for the next few hours, somehow sure that the old sycamore was standing tall and free of its ghost. Before we dozed off, we put our hands together and swore solemnly not to tell anybody else that the ghost was gone.

"Yeah," I said, half asleep. "Let the boys keep on daring each other."

It was months later that I heard a new twist to the sycamore tree ghost legend. Seems young Billy Watson had been coming home late one night, having had quite a bit to drink. He swore he saw not one ghost but lots, half a dozen at least, of white shrouded ghosts weaving their way up the mountainside. Now the tree has a whole family of ghosts to keep the boys daring each other.

Watermelon on the Fourth

AFTER PEEDEE LEFT, the next big excitement of the summer was that I saw Daddy's brother, my uncle William, for the second and last time. He came home from the service on what they called a "furlough." He was tall and quiet and seemed preoccupied. Louise whispered to Annie, "He knows he'll be going overseas and he's not telling his mama."

It was the fourth of July and hot, not a breeze even at the top of the mountain. Daddy had come by himself to Bruton Mountain, Mama being sickly. There was a festive air about the place. Everybody had come up to celebrate William's coming home in his creased uniform and polished boots. But he wouldn't put it back on. Right after he'd thrown his duffel bag down and hugged Grandma, he went to Johnnie's room and changed into his old clothes.

All of us kids were in the back yard, under the walnut tree, eating watermelon. There was a certain edginess in the air because the men had started drinking earlier in the day and the women were disgusted with them. The women were crowded into the hot kitchen and hadn't put the food out on the long tables in the yard yet. Especially Louise was in a stormy mood. We could hear her slamming things around in the kitchen and talking loudly about Jude and men in general.

Nobody had ever said so, but I sensed that Jude was a heavy drinker. Annie's kids were always saying he was mean as a junkyard dog. Jude alternated between staggering through the house, shouting, picking on Louise for being lazy and not getting the food ready and sprawling on the porch, scowling and muttering. The men ignored him and I don't remember a single thing he said or yelled. It didn't make sense and wasn't directed at us kids. At one of his outbursts, aimed at Louise apparently, she yelled right back at him, something else I never heard before or since. He got up and shuffled toward the kitchen, and we heard pans crashing against the wall.

Louise came charging out the back door, headed for the wood shed. Jude followed, gesturing, staggering, shouting incoherently. Louise grabbed a double-headed axe and turned on him. He stopped dead in his tracks. I stopped eating my watermelon and absently swallowed a seed. Jude moved as fast as he could under the circumstances, turning back toward the house. Louise's swing caught him on the hip pocket of his loose overalls—smashing a good fifth of real "bonded in bond" liquor. Blood, glass, and whiskey mingled in Jude's hip pocket, but it was nothing serious. Except that an old hen had taken advantage of my preoccupation and had pecked away all my piece of watermelon.

William saw me staring and winked. "Nice day on the mountain, huh?"

Daddy and Grandpa got Jude by the arms and dragged him around the house where he slept the rest of the day. William shrugged and went to sit under the walnut tree. He lit a cigarette and stared into space. I wanted to go talk to him, but he didn't look like he wanted company. And he left two days later, in his creased pants and polished boots.

Learning about Leonie

GRANDMA AND I smelled Johnnie before we saw him. Johnnie had gone off to the post office because Grandma wanted to hear from her daughter Leonie. Leonie lived in the Piedmont and Grandma said she'd been having some trouble lately, and she'd had Annie write her a letter. Grandma could write, but as she said, "Annie's got the prettiest hand around." Now Grandma was hoping for an answer.

"What kind of trouble?" I'd asked. But Grandma didn't answer me, just looked past me into some place I could not see. Seemed there was a lot of trouble down in the Piedmont. Grandma's silence didn't bother me. I was used to it.

"Do you smell something?" I sniffed the hot August air. I held up the slingshot I was working on and sighted at a fence post. I sniffed again. It was something down the road.

Grandma stopped breaking up half-runner beans. We said it at the same time.

"Skunk."

"There's Johnnie, way down there below the creek," I said. He was in the shadows, but I was sure it was Johnnie. And the stink was coming from his direction.

"Law, law," Grandma said. She stood up and set the dishpan full of beans in her chair. She walked to the edge of the porch and flipped her apron a couple of time. The three chickens that always escaped their chicken lot had been under the floor in the shade and came clucking out to peck at the bean strings.

"I bet some old skunk's got Johnnie!" I craned my neck, but Johnnie was not coming any closer.

"Go get three or four quarts of tomatoes, June. There's bound to be some left from last summer. Get them. Pour them in a bucket and bring them. I'll get some lye soap and some towels." Grandma turned toward the door. "Hurry it up. If we smell him here, you can imagine what he's smelling hisself."

Grandma met me at the edge of the yard. She had clean overalls and a shirt over her arm along with towels and a box of matches in her hand. "Can you carry some water, too, June?"

The smell got worse, the closer we got to Johnnie. He stood in the middle of the road, a few steps beyond the creek that ran across it.

"Lord, Johnnie, you must have riled it," Grandma said.

Johnnie's grin was lopsided because he'd pressed his arm across his face and nose.

"I should have brought me a clothes pin." I said. "You stink awful."

"Don't tease him, June."

"Do I have to take this stuff to him?" I gagged. Grandma held the towels close to her face.

She considered the situation. "Give me the buckets, June. You stay here."

She slipped off her shoes and rolled her stockings down and off and waded through the shallow creek.

"Take off your clothes, Johnnie, and throw'em in a pile at the edge of the road there."

Johnnie didn't move. I pinched my nose with my fingers and breathed through my mouth and squatted down in the road to watch. I'd heard of skunks spraying people but this was as close as I'd ever been to the actual occasion. I breathed into my arms over my knees. The tomatoes had left a little odor on my hands. I concentrated on that.

"You got a letter, Ma," Johnnie said. I could see a strip of white jutting out his pocket.

Grandma stopped several feet from Johnnie. She looked sickly-faced and held a hand across her mouth.

"It stinks, Ma. That skunk sprayed high and got the letter."

The side of the road was a bank of red dirt, three or four feet high. Grandma looked at Johnnie who was holding the letter. "Johnnie, the best thing you can do for that letter now is to bury it. Dig some dirt out of that bank and cover it up. Maybe that'll take the smell out."

Johnnie nodded. He found a flat rock and used it to dig some dirt from the bank and after a few minutes he laid the rock down and put the letter on it. He looked around, and spotted another rock bigger than his two hands put together. He laid that on top and scraped dirt over them until they were covered. His face was screwed up either from the skunk smell or from his careful handling of the task his mother assigned him. I was about to be sick. Still I intended to see what happened.

Johnnie stood up, half in the shadows of the trees above the bank. Grandma looked like she wanted to fall over. "Your clothes have to be burned, Johnnie. Do you hear me? Take them off and scrub down with this bucket of tomatoes. That's all that'll cut that smell. Then lather off good with soap and water. All over. Wash your feet in the creek. Throw your clothes over there and set them on fire. All of them." She breathed into the towels.

"Here's some towels when you're finished. And some clean clothes. I'm leaving them here."

"I ain't gonna take my clothes off," Johnnie said.

"Well, how are you going to burn them?" Grandma never lost patience with Johnnie, but I think she was coming close. She glanced at me.

"You turn yourself around, June. Or go on back to the house."

"I want to stay."

"Well, close your eyes and look the other way." The smell must have been getting to Grandma. But I knew what she meant. Johnnie wasn't going to take off his clothes with me looking.

"I mean it, June."

I turned around and looked toward the house. I couldn't hear what Johnnie muttered, but Grandma said, "She ain't looking and she ain't going to."

I heard the faint clinks of Johnnie's overall galluses coming undone, and I knew I was going to disobey Grandma.

When I sneaked my head around, she was looking at the mound of dirt where the letter was, not at Johnnie and luckily not at me. Johnnie was funny looking out of his clothes, thin and real pale. His face and neck were darker and his hands and feet, but I wasn't looking at them. I was looking at my first naked man, well, boy, well, the first full naked boy body I'd seen outside diapers. It wasn't much to look at, as far as I could see. But I couldn't stare, didn't dare get caught.

So it was just a quick look. Johnnie was scrunched over, sloshing tomatoes and juice on his long arms, then shivering and scrubbing with the towel. He was all splotchy-looking with bits of tomatoes all over him. He was also sun-dappled in the shade. I didn't see what all the fuss was about—all the giggles and whispers I heard when girls talked about boys and their dangling things. Kind of pitiful. I started to turn my head again, to double check.

"June, you heard what I said, young lady." Grandma's voice was sharp. "Plenty of time for you to wonder yet."

"Yes, ma'am." I faced the house until I heard Johnnie strike a match. "Can I look now?"

"You can carry these buckets back to the house, young lady. You've had enough excitement for one day." I could tell it was all right for me to look at the clean Johnnie. He was throwing some brush on the fire. The smell wasn't completely gone, but it was manageable, at least.

"Johnnie, put the towels here in the creek. Weigh them down. The water'll get the smell out."

Johnny had slicked down his hair. He stayed at the fire a while longer after he'd put the towels in the creek. He wouldn't look at me, but I looked straight at him. He looked a lot better with his clothes on.

The slight odor of skunk lingered around the place and around Johnnie for a week or more. I wondered about the letter between the rocks. Grandma eyed the skies every day and I bet she prayed it wouldn't rain. Still the damp dirt couldn't be doing that letter any good. Grandpa didn't know it was there.

When Leonie had left home with just the clothes on her back and the promise of a job in the cotton mill, he said he didn't want to hear her name spoken again in his house. I knew that because one time Daddy forgot and asked about her. "I said I never wanted to hear her name in this house again," Grandpa said. And Grandma didn't answer Daddy. After dinner, they walked out to the edge of the yard to look at the grapevines and they talked a little then.

About a week after the skunk day, Grandpa said, "You're mighty fidgety these days, Woman. Can't a man have some peace in his own house?" She hadn't said a word, and I couldn't see any difference in her behavior except for pausing and staring down the road quite often. She didn't answer Grandpa, just took out her little pocket knife and started tending to a hangnail on her hand.

The next morning was drizzly. Grandpa and Johnnie left early, and Grandma was fidgety till they got out of the house. "Go down and get that letter, June," she told me. Her lumbago had been acting up, especially after wading that creek, and she didn't want to walk any more than she had to. I grabbed the fireplace shovel and ran down the road and dug up the letter. The envelope was pretty messy and I couldn't read even Grandma's name and address.

Grandma took the wet, dirty envelope and went to sit by the kitchen stove. I trailed along curious but not wanting to intrude. She held the letter to the stove for some time, drying it out a little. She didn't notice that her hands were turning red from the heat. I picked up a biscuit from the top of stove and laid a piece of crisp fried meat on it and waited. Grandma finally noticed me when I was getting a drink from the water bucket and when her scorched hands must have hurt.

"It's from Leonie," she said.

I nodded. I'd never met Aunt Leonie except when I was a baby and didn't remember. She was Grandma's oldest girl and a real beauty everybody said.

"Like fine china," Annie had said of her. "And real fragile, too. She'd a-been broke in a thousand pieces if she'd stayed at home." Annie had not said anymore and looked like she shouldn't have said that much. I thought my mama was awfully pretty, but I didn't know about real beauty.

One day, weeks after Annie had revealed that little bit about Leonie, right out of the blue, I asked, "Annie, is my mama a real beauty?" We were hoeing her bean patch and hadn't been talking at all. She leaned on her hoe and wiped her face with her apron.

"With her curly hair and big eyes, your mama's a mighty pretty woman, June, no mistake about that." She stopped and thought some more. "I tell you, if anybody hadn't seen Leonie, they'd call Rose a real beauty. It's hard to put words to it, June. Your mama's as pretty a woman as we see around these parts, but she's a woman and no man ever forgets it. Now Leonie, she's almost like an angel like them pictures you see sometimes on your Sunday school cards."

Annie wiped her face again, smudging it a little. "Bruton's Mountain's no place for angels, June. You got to be tough to survive up here. Leonie was tender as a lamb. She'd a-been broke worst than she is now if she'd a stayed." That was a long speech for Annie and when she went back to hoeing, I didn't ask any more questions. She must have thought I knew a lot about Leonie but I didn't. I wondered about being an angel in the Piedmont.

"I have to read it, I reckon," Grandma said. "I dread to open it."

"Want me to read it to you?"

She handed me the letter. "It still smells a little," I said.

The words were real smeary and I couldn't make out all the letters. "Dear Mama," I read.

Grandma's head was bowed low toward her lap. She'd stuck her hands together like the picture of Jesus at prayer and she looked at them, not at me as I read. "...my first and last letter to you...not Pa. They say I done it...soon...if I can...doctor testified... baby boy."

I glanced at Grandma. Now her fingers were laced together hard so that her knuckles showed white. "I can't make it all out," I said. "Looks like a name next, maybe Linc...Lincoln?" Grandma waited. I read on. "Linc...to Texas...west. Don't tell....letter. I ...disappear...and...don't worry, Mama. I don't think I did what they ...care of Johnnie...Love..." I stopped. "She didn't sign it," I said, "but there's some big X's here for kisses, I guess."

Grandma held out her hand and I put the letter in it. Aunt Leonie was more a mystery now than ever. Grandma laid the letter on her lap and took out her handkerchief and blew her nose. She looked at the damp letter a long time. Then she took the envelope I handed her and opened the stove eye. She didn't wad them up, just placed both pieces of paper on the small fire and we watched them blaze up and turn to black and fall among the coals.

"I don't want you ever mentioning this letter, June. You hear?"

I nodded. I wouldn't ever want to say anything that would make Grandma look so sad again. "Not even to Annie," she said. I nodded again.

I was too big to sit on Grandma's lap, but I wandered to the back of her chair and put my hand on the gray bun at the back of her head.

"I hate the smell of skunk," I said. Grandma put her hand on mine, awkwardly. Then she stood up.

"Me too," she said. "Let's go look at my grapevines, June. They're coming along. This rain's good for them."

Paraphernalia

IN EARLY AUGUST Grandma was talking to the post master outside the church. He introduced us to his daughter and his son-in-law, and their girl Marsha who was my age. Before I knew it, I was invited to go with Mr. and Mrs. Warren and Marsha to see "Unto These Hills" in Cherokee. I couldn't believe Grandma had said yes, but I heard the post master say something about Marsha didn't have any kids to talk to and something about a "cultural experience." They promised to deliver me back to Flo's by midnight.

Off we went the very next day in the Warrens' fine new Buick, a light blue, the first car I saw that wasn't black. Mr. Warren talked differently, being from New Jersey or Poland or some such place. And he said he didn't like bologna or cornbread. I was in my best dress and new shoes, my hair combed back and my fingernails clean. I couldn't think of much to say to Marsha the whole way out there.

At the parking lot, we were expected to leave the car, and walk up the mountain to the site of the performance. Mr. Warren, who was in his stout forties, was having none of this walking bit. The day was hot, the road looked steep. Others were trudging upward in twos and threes. The uniformed attendant who materialized from somewhere threw up his hand and Mr. Warren had to stop. He looked impressive to us girls in the back seat. He wore a holster. Probably he was also a local policeman. It was a day of newness for me—my first parking attendant. But he seemed less impressed with the baby blue Buick with its eight portholes than I was.

"Nope. Can't drive up. Space up there reserved for the company and the press. You'll have to park in the regular lot. You can turn around there" He waved to a wide place in the road and pointed back down the hill. Mr. Warren had already ignored the big sign that clearly said "Parking beyond this point prohibited" and the flimsy barricade. By judicious steering, he had gotten the big car on the other side and we were about a third of the way up the hill.

Mrs. Warren looked only slightly daunted, and her husband looked as if the man were a plowboy rather than a uniformed and armed representative of the theater company and the law. Marsha and I leaned forward, attentive as storybook mice. I sensed a confrontation even if I didn't know the word. Mr. Warren squared his shoulders, in a white linen sports jacket (also the first time I'd seen that on a man—and a dark blue shirt with splashy green and yellow designs).

"My good man," he started, and his wife said at the same time, "My dear fellow..."

I thought to myself, people really do talk like that—outside of books? I waited.

"Turn around sir," the man said. He was sweating in the sun, and was in the act of producing a handkerchief to dry his forehead. "Everybody wants to drive up. Save theirselfs the long walk. Everybody's got to park down there." He emphasized "down" and again pointed in that direction, just in case we weren't sure of our ups and downs.

Mr. Warren fixed the man with a stare and said, "We are not everybody."

Mrs. Warren said, touching his arm, "George."

The man wiped his neck with his handkerchief. "The only people driving up this here mountain is PRESS people."

Mr. Warren reached into his back pocket and took out his wallet. He showed the man something, some sort of ID. He had told me he'd been a photographer in the Merchant Marines and probably had all kinds of ID cards available. And, in fact, the trunk was full of camera equipment in tin cases.

The man looked both uncomfortable and adamant. We were getting hotter in the back seat, and I was squirming a little so I didn't hear all the next words, but I plainly heard the word that made the difference.

"Can't carry all this damn paraphernalia up this hill in this heat."

I was now looking straight at the sweating man, and I knew instantly that when that big word—paraphernalia—the first time I ever heard it—hit him, he had lost. He stepped back as if the word were an arrow that had punctured his authority, and left it leaking. Before he could lose any more, he gave in with the relief that comes when a higher power has spoken and he's no longer in charge.

"Yes sir," he said. "Go on up, then."

Mr. Warren put the car into gear again, and we eased on upward, passing the people who were merely walking.

"What's parifnalia?" Marsha asked.

"Stuff, honey," her father said. "Just a lot of stuff."

She settled back, content. But the encounter was like a revelation to me. I had seen the power of words, specifically of a word. A good word, a big word could make a southern law enforcement officer let a Yankee drive on up the hill when everything in him wanted to put him in his place, which was someplace up north. A well-chosen word meant riding rather than walking in the hot August sun. I savored the word. I said it under my breath. I couldn't wait till it was my turn to use it.

Watson's Old Ram

PEEDEE'S BROTHERS WERE generally known as "rapscallions" by the respectable members of our Piney Fork Free Will Baptist Church. I figured that word meant the boys were always getting into trouble but people liked them anyway and enjoyed recounting their exploits. PeeDee herself did not talk much about her family at all. Her mother seemed to shift between being overbearing and being passive and withdrawn; she didn't have many friends. Partly that was because the family moved a lot and Mr. Rednell didn't like to work.

But her brothers kept the tongues wagging. One time Marvin got Johnnie in trouble. Marvin came across the mountain to see if Johnnie could help out at the Watsons where the Rednells were living and helping with the crops. Johnnie came back home in disgrace, according to Annie who told Mama all about it when they came to get me at the end of the summer. I was listening, hanging on to every word.

"That Marvin, he's likely to come to no good end," Annie started the tale. She and Mama were rocking before the fire in Annie's living room. I had come down the mountain to meet them and so Daddy had gone on up the mountain to visit for awhile. We had stayed at Annie's to keep warm and gossip. Mama declared that the road was too muddy and the wind too chilly to go any further. Daddy was relieved to go alone. He was worried lately about his mama and daddy, I could tell.

"What's Marvin done now?" Mama asked.

"He's to blame for Mr. Watson's prize ram being just about dead, may be dead by now." Annie spit discretely into a coffee can she put to her lips. Mama glanced aside. That was one habit Mama could not abide. Using snuff. She didn't seem to mind as much when Grandma and other older women poked fingerfulls of snuff in the back of their mouth or a few of them in between their gum and lower lip, but every time a young woman like Annie spit, Mama winced and turned aside. It was the only thing she didn't like about Annie. Annie knew Mama didn't like it. I heard her say one time, "Talk all you want about the habit, but when it's about the only thing to give you pleasure—"

She broke off. Mama had looked strangely at her. "Robert—don't you—?"

Both of them saw me getting a drink of water from the bucket. I put the dipper back as the silence lengthened. I went out of the room, but I heard Annie say, "Robert's gone most of the time, and when he's here, he's in a hurry or dead tired."

I heard Mama sigh in some kind of agreement.

"That ram's Joe Watson's pride and joy," Mama said. "What in the world did Marvin do?"

"Him and Johnnie tied the Watson's old collie to that ram's back last spring--"

"That must have been a sight! I thought nobody could get near the creature."

"You know Johnnie's got a way with animals. Even that mean old ram. Johnnie helped Marvin get that collie on the ram's back. It scared him to death, just about. That ram took off across the pasture just a-flying. The collie was clawing, holding on, the rope was a-slipping."

Annie wiped her eyes with her hand. Mama laughed out loud. Annie went on, "I guess it's not all that funny, but just picturing it gets me going every time. Anyway, the ram must have run all over that field. The rope slipped and that collie swung under its belly and then it really took off. The boys were trying to catch it. So they's making it worse, scaring it even more. They must have run it for a long time. It finally had to slow down and one of them, Johnnie, caught up and pulled it down to the ground. It was a-panting and wheezing for dear life."

Here they laughed again. "Any damage done?" Mama asked, and they really laughed.

"That old ram's been taking it easy for awhile, I reckon," Annie said. "The boys got the collie untied. It's got a broke foot, I hear, from where the ram rolled on him. They can't get that dog anywhere near the sheep lot. They say he even lays his ears back when Johnnie comes near him, and Johnnie's always liked that old dog."

"How'd Joe Watson find out?" Mama wondered.

"I heard he went looking for the ram later that day, and he was still resting up in the pasture, plum tuckered out. And the boys forgot to take the rope with them. It was right next to the ram."

"And the collie's foot?" Mama interjected.

"Yeah, that too," Annie sobered. "Joe Watson sent Johnnie home with orders to stay there, called him an idiot for listening to Marvin. I don't know what Mr. Bruton done to Johnnie. You know he can be mean as a snake sometimes. I hope he didn't give Johnnie a beating."

"Likely did," Mama said. "That man's got a temper. If he didn't thrash Johnnie, chances are he went after Joe Watson for calling Johnnie names."

"Your man'll find out, I guess," Annie said. "I heard the story from Kate Alston over at the post office, didn't hear it from anybody on this mountain."

"One of these days Marvin is going to go too far," Mama predicted. "He's getting too big for his britches and his daddy's too drunk most of the time to care what he's doing."

"He's a rapscallion all right," Annie agreed. "But lord, that ram must've been a sight to see!"

1944-45 FALL AND WINTER TURNING COLD

Mama—Just Passing Through

MAMA WAS THE boss in our family. She was the "outsider," being from Georgia and all. That's what someone at church said one time, "Well, what can you expect? Her being from Georgia and all."

She was only nineteen when she married Daddy. She'd been to Atlanta and even to the ocean. She plucked her eyebrows, and sometimes she came back from Sylva with fingernail polish. While Daddy sharpened tools in the evening by the fire and I read or did my numbers, Mama painted her nails. I'd watch her hold her fingers before her and carefully blow on them to dry. Sometimes her breath came out more like a sigh, delicate, hardly disturbing the air currents, but I noticed. Daddy was proud of her curly blond hair and her slimness. Anybody could see that. Once Uncle Cade remarked to Daddy, "She sure keeps you on a short leash," and Daddy laughed, "She's right feisty."

She did all the things women did around the house, but Mama was different. It was like she was a stranger passing through the community, just biding her time.

Mama baked biscuits and cornbread, she canned green beans and made kraut every summer, she sewed, making my dresses, and she cleaned. But all these daily acts she performed as if she was in someone else's home. Or as if she didn't expect the house to be there when she returned from a day away. There was a restlessness in her eyes that Annie or Louise didn't have. But she couldn't just leave, having left her family which in

99

turn had left Georgia and gone across the country to settle in the state of Washington. She had no money and she had me.

Nothing Daddy did quite measured up to Mama's expectations. He cut cabbage during the summer and he worked in the kraut canning factory when it was operating. He worked for other men who had farms requiring a strong body. Sometimes he helped Grandpa with the logging. He was always working, often gone during the week and reappearing on Friday nights. He looked bone tired by the time he was thirty. I heard whispers about other reasons he was so tired, that Mama just wore him out.

One Sunday after I'd come back from Bruton's Mountain and just after school started, I cut my foot badly. I was playing ball over at the Blantons and I ran into the weeds after an easy fly and stepped on a broken beer bottle. I'd been told I could stay all day at the Blantons and even eat supper with them. But Mrs. Blanton had gone somewhere, and I decided to go on home instead of bleeding in their yard. I dawdled a little, stopping at the branch to watch the stream turn red as my foot turned numb in the cold water. I tied the old towel back on my foot and got to our house. I was feeling faint and was surprised to see the door open. I thought Mama had gone visiting that day. Mrs. Hall was just leaving.

"What happened to you?" Mrs. Hall was sharp tongued and usually sharp-eyed. Since any fool could see I'd cut my foot, I hobbled past her up the steps which she looked as if she were guarding and went straight to Mama. She was sitting propped up on the bed, a light blanket across her although it must have been eighty degrees. I stuck my foot up on the edge of the bed for her to admire the blood. She was pale and sickly looking, her hair damp around the edges. She turned her head to the side. Mrs. Hall was right behind me. She hustled me into the front room, her hand clamped on my shoulder. Out of the corner of my eye, I saw that the kitchen was a big mess. She must have been washing sheets and towels for Mama, and it not even Monday.

"Leave your Mama alone, June. Put your foot up on this chair and stay right here." She brought a pan of hot water and a clean rag from the kitchen. "Come here. Let me clean that."

Mama didn't say anything. She just kept her head turned, like she didn't want to see me. I wanted her to wash my foot, not Mrs. Hall. But I sat on the floor, my foot up on the chair. Mrs. Hall's hands were gentle as she massaged my foot to bring fresh blood oozing out.

"That'll help to clarify the wound," she said. She swabbed the ell-shaped gash with Mercurochrome and tied a clean white cloth over the foot. I wasn't about to cry in front of her, but I had to grit my teeth.

"You better keep shoes on for a day or two. And stay off the foot," she said. "That's deep. You don't want to get it infected."

"I have to get in the wood and carry in water."

"Your daddy will be home. He can do that."

"He's gone now till next Friday."

"He'll be here directly," Mrs. Hall said. "You stay off that foot. And don't go bothering your mama. She's doing poorly."

She was right. Daddy came home that very day. Rushing in. Went right to Mama. I don't think he even noticed my foot until I propped it on a kitchen chair. That was much later after he'd fried us some eggs and potatoes and made cornbread fritters on top of the stove. I was reading a story from *Grimm's Fairy Tales* about a girl and a frog. Daddy wasn't much of a cook, but he knew where the forks and spoons were and not to leave a towel right on the hot stove. Mama didn't get up that day and half the next.

Daddy stayed home and did the cooking and all the work around the house. He dropped the bottle of Mercurochrome and it broke, spreading a red stain on the kitchen floor. Daddy gagged at the sight. Then he swabbed my foot with kerosene and packed a piece of fatback on it. "This'll draw the poison out," he told me.

"I've got to get out of here," I heard Mama say to Daddy a few days later. My foot still throbbed and hurt so that I wanted to cry, but Mama was so quiet and far away that I didn't want to bother her. I stayed on the porch in the sunshine most of the day, watching my foot heal. Daddy even brought me a fried baloney sandwich out for lunch.

I dozed in the sunshine, concentrating on the throbbing in my foot until the rhythm became a kind of hum and then I'd nap. But I heard them talking.

"I can't stay in this house another week. Why can't you understand that?" Mama said.

"Rose, I can't find us another house just like that."

"You can try, can't you? You've not been trying."

"What with taking care of you and June—" Daddy paused a long time. "How much time have I had this week?"

"Well, get out and find us somewhere else to live." Mama's voice was shrill. "I can't stand it here! Not after—"

"Keep your voice down. June's on the porch. Sleeping. Don't wake her up."

"June this! June that! I'm the one you should be concerned about," Mama yelled.

"I'll go talk to Snyder down at the store. He might know someplace we could get. It's not easy..."

"Just go and do it, Carl. All I hear from you is excuses. I don't care if we have to live in a log cabin! I'm getting out of this house."

"June's got neighbor kids to play with here," Daddy said. "She likes it here. I don't know if there's any place—"

"June'll be all right wherever we move. Carl, don't come back till you've found us a place. I mean it." The bedsprings squeaked as Mama sat down heavily. "I mean it," she said again. The tone of her voice sent little shivers up me.

When Daddy came out, I pretended to be sleeping. The break in his stride told me he stopped and looked at me, or at least he stopped. I heard his steps off the porch and watched him walk toward the road. I knew Daddy would find us another house.

Indian Turnip

"DON'T GO WANDERING off, now!" PeeDee spoke sharply to her younger sister.

They were both at my house for the day, which was unusual. PeeDee didn't like to be responsible for her younger sisters. She said it never failed that she'd get into trouble when they were under her care. But PeeDee had begged her father to leave her off to visit with me on his way into town that spring Saturday. He had refused until she said she'd even bring Lily, who was four years old. Her mother was feeling "puny" and had prevailed on Mr. Rednell to agree. He left them in our front yard, not even a greeting to me.

"I'll be here by five. Be ready." The two girls nodded. So we had the rest of the morning and all afternoon to ourselves.

"We've got almost seven hours to kill," PeeDee announced. "You can finish reading *Little Women* to me, to us."

For a few minutes every time we were together for the past three weeks, which hadn't been much, I'd been reading the story out loud. PeeDee could read, of course, but she preferred to hear the story, rather than read it herself. We savored the details of family life, and we predicted the outcome of the family fortunes. She made me promise not to read ahead while she was not there, and I didn't. But that was a hard promise to keep. We both wanted the book to last on and on, but I also wanted to know the whole story right then. When it came to reading, PeeDee had a lot more patience than I did. So while I was waiting to continue *Little Women*, I was also reading, really struggling to understand the sentences in *David Copperfield*.

Mama was resting in the back bedroom where it was cool and dark. She hadn't been feeling good lately and she was snappish at the slightest thing. I knew she wanted Daddy to find another house for us and she was impatient. My foot was still sore from that deep cut, and I was limping so PeeDee was right. It was a good day for reading.

"Mama, can I fix us something to eat? We're going to sit under the walnut tree and read."

She wasn't exactly happy to have two more girls underfoot, but I'd told her when I went in to announce I had company that we'd not bother her. We'd be quiet and stay out of the house. She barely raised her head. "See what you can find. Whatever's on the stove."

I got six biscuits and slathered them with some of Aunt Mattie's apple butter and took the three slices of leftover bacon from the warmer.

"Let's go," I announced. "Here, Lily, I'll pour you some milk." I gave her a big enamel cup and we filled it up at the springhouse where the milk stayed cool.

For an hour or so, we occupied ourselves with eating and finding mica. Finding chips of mica was a favorite pastime. Somewhere we'd gotten the idea that we could make lots of money if we could just get enough of the shiny stuff. We spent a lot of time with our eyes down, peering at rocks. I had a mayonnaise jar almost half full already.

I opened *Little Women* to read. Lily listened for maybe ten minutes. Then she became restless. First, she kept interrupting until PeeDee snapped at her. She examined her toes and her scabs on her legs for a few minutes. Then she turned or tried to turn a few somersaults, demanding that we look at her each time. We were right in the middle of Mrs. March's sickness, and Lily wasn't properly attentive.

The walnut tree we leaned against was quite a ways from our house. We'd cut through our garden patch and were actually on Mr. Meister's property. Beyond was a scraggly pasture now empty of cows and full of thistles. Through the pasture ran a trickle of a stream. It was overgrown now, so the water was hardly visible and not even ankle deep at this time of the year.

Lily's sharp eyes, though, had spotted water and she was interested.

"I'm going to play in the water." She pointed across the field.

"No, you're not," PeeDee contradicted her. "You'll get dirty and Daddy will blame me."

"Going. Going!" Lily's eyes started brimming over. "You can't stop me."

"Let her go, PeeDee," I said. "We can watch her from here. There's no cows in the pasture. She'll be all right."

"Well, go on, but keep your dress clean," PeeDee said. "And don't go wandering off."

We were conscientious. At the end of every paragraph, we looked up and checked on Lily. She took a long time just getting to the water, stopping to admire every mossy rock and every thistle in the pasture. The afternoon was as quiet as a sick room, and probably both of us were in that sickroom at the March family home when Lily's screams pulled us back to the walnut tree and reality. Lily was toddling toward us, crying. We ran to see what was wrong.

"Lord, I hope she's not snake bit!" PeeDee said.

Lily's face was swelling up and she could hardly talk. Tears rolled down her face.

"What happened? Did you get snake bit?"

She shook her head no. She clutched something in her hand and wiped her lips with the other. "I can't breathe good," she gasped.

"Did you eat something? Did you eat this?" PeeDee picked up Lily and we started back to our house, PeeDee far ahead. I couldn't put much weight on my cut foot, so I hobbled along behind.

"Mrs. Bruton, Mrs.Bruton, come quick. Lily's dying or something!" PeeDee dumped her sister on the front porch and pounded on the door.

Mama came out just as I got to the yard. She took one look at Lily and paled. "What in the world's wrong with her?"

Lily's face was swollen more. She could barely whisper. "I ate this onion." She let the green stalk fall to the porch.

"June, run get your daddy's mother's doctor book."

PeeDee was holding her sister's head in her lap. Lily didn't look too good. I didn't know what we could do. Daddy was not at home or anywhere close by. Our nearest neighbors had left that morning going to Macon County to visit. I couldn't run the several miles to the next neighbors, nor could Mama. PeeDee could, but Lily was clinging to her with both hands and breathing hard.

"Look up Indian turnip, hurry," instructed Mama. She looked too pale and faint to do much. My fingers were clumsy, but I found it.

"Says here to use raw eggs and cream and some melted lard." I put the book in Mama's hands. "Here, I'll go get the stuff."

I cracked three eggs in the big mixing bowl and poured all our cream and a little milk in. I dipped out a big spoonful of lard and blew on the coals to make the fire come alive. I put the lard in a pan right over the coals and it melted pretty quick. I had put the eggs and cream on the stove so they were slightly warm. All the time, I heard PeeDee comforting her sister as best she could, and Mama saying over and over, "Lord a-mercy, Lord a-mercy." She got a quilt from the house and covered Lily who couldn't speak but was breathing a little.

I took the concoction to the front porch. Lily didn't want to open her mouth, but PeeDee pried it open and I got a spoonful of the stuff into her mouth. She couldn't swallow it. Mama knelt beside her and stroked her swollen neck.

"Keep pouring it in, June. PeeDee, keep her mouth open as best you can." Mama gagged at the mess we made, the milky yellow concoction dribbling down Lily's face, but she kept frantically stoking her throat. PeeDee smeared the dribbles around on Lily's face. She was a mess. We worked on her almost an hour. She didn't seem to be getting any worse, but her eyes were closed, pinched up and she couldn't talk. We got most of the mixture into her.

"Run for old Mrs. Hall," Mama told PeeDee. "She's going to make it, I think, but we don't know what might happen."

"I'll hold her," I told PeeDee. "She's okay, now. Look, she breathing almost regular."

Before PeeDee got back with Mrs. Hall and before Mr. Rednell came, I carried Lily into the living room and put her on the bed in the corner. Mrs. Hall brought some herbs with her and made a hot tea.

"Get her to drink this every three or four hours," Mrs. Hall told PeeDee. "It'll make her throat open up, but it'll take a week or more." She handed Mr. Rednell the half gallon jar. "A spoonful of honey'll make it go down better."

Mr. Rednell smelled just slightly of alcohol, but he thanked her for her help. He didn't even look at Mama. I thought Grandma's doctor book and Mama's stroking of Lily's throat had saved her. Lily's lips were swollen but she was quiet. I knew she was going to make it, and she did.

PeeDee told me later, weeks later, that her father didn't speak the whole way home, and he beat her with a razor strap for not watching over Lily. He told her, "If Lily'd died, I'd have killed you." No wonder PeeDee didn't like to be in charge of her sisters.

Hog Killing Time

IT WAS A cold November day. The fine dry snow that blew through the air lay lightly on the ground. Even in the kitchen with a wood fire going in the stove—as it had been all day—I was chilly from the draft under the door. I was at the end of the kitchen table, too far away from the fire. We had a bunch of company from Bruton's Mountain. My mother and Grandma, closer to the stove, were perspiring lightly. It was hog killing day.

I'd come home from school to find the kitchen in a bustle of activity. The small kitchen held only a stove, a counter built along one side with shelves above, and a table with six straight chairs. The counter was where vegetables were chopped and the biscuits or cornbread stirred up. A curtain strung around it concealed utensils, pots, pans, jugs, extra cans. The kitchen smelled of work, of bustle, of steady, keep going work; it smelled of soap suds and ashes and faintly of Grandma's snuff. It smelled mostly, though, of fresh meat, of blood hardly congealed, of something too close to the source. It also smelled of fat, pure and simple. All afternoon the two women had rearranged the family hog that had been shot early that morning and been "worked over" by the men out doors.

Johnnie and one of Jude's boys had come to help with the day's work. They had wrestled the hog to the ground or clubbed it with a lucky blow as they chased it in the lot. They then got out of the way and let one of the grownups use the rifle to put one bullet in the brain, a bullet that had to strike cleanly--or should. They'd been engaged for a couple of hours after the killing in hauling the carcass up on a contraption of poles, so the blood could drain after the throat was slit. We didn't save the blood, but some families didn't waste a bit, and used the blood for pudding. The scraping of the bristles was a tedious job and one the boys usually did. They kept the fire going and the pot filled with water. Boiling water softened the tough hide so it could be scraped more easily.

So the men and boys worked in the freezing weather, most without gloves, some without caps, all without scarves. Their work pants and overalls were filthy, blood crusted, and slick with grease by the time the hog was properly chopped up. Through the morning, the boys supplied them with hot coffee and offers of a biscuit. They drank the coffee and shook their heads at the thought of food. Before noon, usually by eleven o'clock, they had done their part and were ready for dinner. Hams still had to be salted and prepared, and some cleaning up had to be done, but now it was Mama and Grandma's turn.

They'd been getting things ready, and they may already have started on the inside "working up" of the hog. But certainly they had mid-day dinner ready: leather britches and cornbread, cabbage fried in fatback, potato salad or mashed potatoes or fried potatoes, plenty of coffee and buttermilk. They'd likely serve a blackberry cobbler from the berries picked and canned in the summer, with plenty of butter.

The men and boys ate mostly in silence, hunched over their plates. Grandpa poured his coffee into his saucer to cool it and slurped it mightily.

The men could afford to feel good; they pushed their chairs back. Daddy lit a cigarette and Grandpa and Jude's boy cut off a chew of tobacco. They got up periodically to go to the door and spit over the porch into the yard. The back porch showed a tiny line in the snow like a line of little bitty ants making their way from door to yard. But the men didn't linger over their meal. They were fed and out of the kitchen in less than an hour. Mama hated this time of year and the hog killing, but she and Grandma had their work to do.

I watched Mama's awkward movements as she chopped the hog and put it in a large dishpan. Grandma stood at the sausage grinder. This mechanism was screwed securely to the edge of the table. She picked up a double handful of meat, dumped it into the top of the grinder, wiped her right hand briefly on her apron so she could better grip the handle, and bent slightly forward, and turned the handle methodically, not too fast or two slow. I admired her steadiness, her doggedness.

I looked out the window, toward the road that wound up the hill. Somebody was walking fast, almost trotting, toward the house. A car or truck could not get to the house right now. Recent hard rains had washed out the road and it had frozen and thawed a couple of times, leaving it impossible to navigate in a vehicle. I could see our visitor was Mr. Sutton from down on the highway. Why was he puffing toward our place?

In a few minutes, he knocked at the door. I wondered why he didn't go around to the back of the house. Surely he saw the smoke and smelled the gore of hog killing time, surely he heard the sounds of the men and boys. He'd know the women were in the house. My mother turned at the sound of knocking. She threw a quick glance at Grandma, whose hands were globbed full of ground meat. "Oh Lord," Grandma said.

"It's probably somebody wanting Mr. Bruton to work," Mama said. She doused her hands in a pan of soapy water and dried them on her apron. I started to get up and go to the door. We wouldn't want to leave anybody standing out in the cold for long. She motioned for me to stay put.

"I'll get it," she said. She dropped her apron on the chair as she left the room. I bit my lower lip. I didn't like the look on her face. It was only old Mr. Sutton, after all. A shaft of cold air hit me as she opened the front door. He said something in a low voice. Then I heard a kind of thump as my mother sat down hard in the rocking chair. I heard it squeak once, but she wasn't rocking.

Grandma dumped the sausage on the table, right on the oilcloth, not even aiming for the dishpan to her right. I gaped at her. She went to the front room, her hands still greasy, little pieces of raw meat still on them.

I heard Mr. Sutton say, "I'm sorry to bring the bad news, Mrs. Bruton."

I got up and looked in the living room. My mother in the rocking chair, not moving. Grandma extending her greasy hand for the telegram. Mr. Sutton standing rigid. He saw me. "Run get your daddy and granddaddy," he said. "Be quick about it!"

I wasn't supposed to go out to where the hog was killed, so when I opened the back door and started down the steps, Daddy knew something was wrong. He and Grandpa came toward me. "Git back in the house, young'un. It's freezing cold out here." They brushed by me. In the kitchen, I shivered as I heard Mr. Sutton say, "It's William. He's been killed in action."

I remembered my uncle William and that hot July on the mountain. He'd winked at me, unhappy looking as he was.

I didn't go into the front room, not even when I heard Mr. Sutton leave. The men stayed in there for awhile. Grandpa and Daddy were talking a little, but not the women. Daddy came in and poured two cups of strong coffee. He took a quart jar from behind some pots behind the curtain and poured a little clear liquid in both cups. I thought it was for him and Grandpa, but I heard him say, "Drink this. Come on. It'll help." There was silence, and then he said roughly, "Drink this, Ma. Do as I say."

In a few minutes, Daddy came back to the kitchen where Johnnie, Jude's boy, and I sat. He said, "You boys go down and sleep at the Boyds tonight. See if Mrs. Boyd can come over and finish this up."

Grandma appeared in the door, Mama pale as a sheet behind her. "No," Grandma said. "We'll do it." She set the coffee cup down on the table. She sounded shaky. "Mrs. Boyd's not one for making good sausage."

She reached over and lifted the glob of meat from the oilcloth and dumped it into the dishpan.

Grandpa came in and picked up the jar of moonshine. By sundown he was drunk and muttering curses in the bedroom. Daddy, whom I had never seen take a drop of alcohol, had poured a pint jar half full and slumped in the living room. Long after dark, long after I had carried in wood for the fire and water for the washing up, Mama and Grandma kept working, not talking at all, grinding, shaping the sausage into patties, frying the patties, stuffing them into jars. They poured hot grease into the blue-tinted jars and, to seal them by congealing, they screwed on lids and turned the jars upside down and lined them up in orderly rows on the table.

A Bad Snow

I STOOD WATCHING the snowflakes drift to the ground. At first the warmer ground devoured them. But in sheer numbers and with the growing cold as the afternoon waned, the ground gave way, the snow prevailed, and before dark a white coverlet disguised the grassless yard, the old wagon wheel, the engine parts, the roofless dog house--all left by the recent renters and inherited by us after Mama insisted on moving. Daddy was working somewhere and had not had time to even pick up around the house, and it was ugly--until the snow came. It was late December, Friday.

"What is so everlasting interesting out there, June?" Mama didn't sound like she expected an answer. I didn't say anything. My eyes followed the descent of a single flake until it mingled with the whiteness.

"Looks to me like you'd have better things to do than just stand there. Have you brought in the wood? Is the water bucket full?" Even though I'd lugged in wood to the kitchen and onto the back porch while she washed our supper dishes and the two water buckets plus the dishpan were filled, the reprimand made me feel guilty.

"It's all done, Mama." I turned around to face her. "And I've done all my homework, too."

Mama was brushing her hair, occasionally taking up the hand mirror to review her work. Sometimes when just the two of us were in the house I wanted to sit close to her, not on her lap. I was too big for that. But she never by look or word invited my closeness. The house was too small for us both. If I stayed in the front room, I was intruding. If I sat at the kitchen table and read or did my arithmetic, she acted as if I was in the way. So when Daddy was gone, we occupied separate houses in a way, coming together only for eating. Now she stretched and yawned.

"Your daddy likely won't be home tonight." She squinted at a reddened spot on her forehead. "They're dead set to finish up that job on Cabin Creek, though how they can work in this weather, I don't know."

"Oh."

"We'll just have to get along without him, I guess." She brushed her hair again.

"I miss him," I said.

That was the wrong thing to say. Just as I turned back to the window, I heard a crash. Mama had thrown the mirror across the room. It hit the wall but didn't break and now it bounced on the floor. I stared at it. That was a practically new mirror.

"You're your daddy's girl, all right. What does he care about us? About me! He ought to be home now—"

I picked up the mirror and put it on the table beside her. She ignored it and bit her lip. She always wore lipstick, but I noticed her lips were a little chapped.

I defended Daddy. "He has to work. The rent's due on this house." I had heard Mr. Barker say we could go ahead and move in but the rent was due the minute Daddy got paid. "Or you'll be out of here, Bruton, if I don't get my rent. I got no axe to grind with you personally, and I hear you're good as your word. Had to haul the last people's stuff out of here myself while they's gone to her papa's, and I dumped it all at the end of the road."

Mr. Barker was as old as the hills and as rough as two roosters fighting, according to Mrs. Hall. His words scared me. I didn't want to think of our things being piled up on the frozen ground at the end of Pounding Mill Branch. Mama had stuck her tongue out at him when his back was turned, but when I grinned at her, she glared and started dragging the mattresses in. Daddy assured Mr. Barker that he'd have his money, he could count on it, and he hurried to help Mama.

Mama had wanted to move, but then she got mad because all of a sudden we had to find a place in a hurry. The Meisters were really sorry to lose us because Daddy helped Mr. Meister out around the place. But their third daughter and four children moved back to Jackson County at Thanksgiving. Her husband was in the CCCs somewhere out west. They wouldn't all fit into the Meisters' house so they had first dibs on the place we rented.

"I thought you'd be happy to leave," Daddy said. "Anyway, blood's thicker than water, Rose. They can't let their own family go to the poor house."

THE SNOW FELL steadily, and I leaned on the cold window sill until it was pitch black dark. Then I took a kerosene lamp and went into the back bedroom. It was cold in there. The rest of the house had tar paper on the outside and the front room and kitchen had boards covering the studs. This little tacked-on room had no tar paper outside or boards inside. Snow could come in through the cracks in the wall. I took a quilt and hung it up on the wall to keep the draft out. There were nails all along the wall for hanging up clothes or pictures and I managed to get the quilt up without making much noise.

I got into bed with all my clothes on and piled the covers over me. I wanted to finish the book I was reading. I held the book with one hand and kept the other one warm under the covers until time to turn the page, then switched hands. My breath showed in the lamp light and my nose was cold, but *Ivanhoe* was so exciting I didn't want to stop.

"June, put that lamp out now and go to sleep." Mama put her head in the doorway. "There's at least three inches already," she said. "Don't waste any more oil. Blow that lamp out."

"Okay." I read more quickly and was at the end of a chapter when she yelled again. "If I have to come in there, I'll blister you."

I skimmed the page and blew out the lamp. In the totally dark room I imagined I could hear the snow fall.

Mama was up before I was, just after the sun glistened across the snow. She broke the ice in the water bucket and made coffee. I washed my face and hands in the icy water and started to set the table. Mama drank black coffee.

"Put lots of milk in yours, if you're bound to drink it," she told me. I felt very grown up with the coffee mug warming my hands. "The biscuits will be ready in a few minutes," she said. "I'm not hungry." She eyed the snow over the rim of the cup.

"You can barely get to the outhouse," she said. "It will be almost up to your knees. We'll be stuck in here all day, looks like."

In a few minutes I came back in and stuck my wet shoes next to the stove. "Reckon Daddy will get home?" I stirred oatmeal into water on the stove, welcoming the warmth as I stood close.

"Who knows what your daddy will do—him and his job." Mama stared out the curtainless window and banged the cup down on the table. "I wish I had a cigarette." She had started smoking after Uncle William's death, and when she was especially irritable she craved a cigarette. "Set some more water on the stove to heat, June. I may wash my hair."

"Your hair's pretty, Mama." I shivered as I lifted the heavy iron kettle full of water to the stove. I hoped she didn't want me to wash my hair on this cold day.

"Pretty dirty, feels like."

The snow had stopped in the night, but before noon it began once more. Besides making up my bed, sweeping, and cleaning up the kitchen, we couldn't do much in the house. And we couldn't do anything outside. At least we didn't have chickens or a hog or a cow to feed. Mama sat and looked out the window and then she walked from room to room. We made a fire in the front room but the stove didn't draw right, so we kept the fire going but not strong. She kept moving around all morning, picking up things and setting them back down. I stayed in the kitchen mostly, with my chair close to the stove. Every time Mama came into the kitchen, I shifted slightly because I was in the way.

"I'm going crazy, cooped up like this," she said. "Carl's not going to get home today."

"Can I make us some snow cream, Mama?" I didn't want to disturb the stillness. But I did like snow cream.

"If you want some, go ahead. Just don't make more than you can eat, don't waste the sugar."

Mama ate four or five spoonfuls of snow cream, but even that didn't distract her. I wished she could sit quietly like Grandma and sew or maybe read. Grandma and I often sat for hours without saying more than a few words. Maybe Mama was missing Daddy and worrying about him.

We ate biscuits and fried potatoes and left-over chicken legs in the middle of the day. The water stayed warm on the back of the stove all day, and Mama bent over a tub to wash her hair. I poured warm water over her head to rinse away the shampoo. She spent an hour or so drying her curly hair and brushing it. I thought maybe that flurry of activity would settle her down. But it didn't.

"June, I'm going down the road to the Suttons. Maybe one of them will take me to the store." She came out of their bedroom with her coat on.

"Mama! It's too cold to go out. Your head's still damp. It's snowing harder. It's a long ways—"

"Oh, June. I'm going. You'll be all right here. Somebody's got to keep the fire going." She sounded relieved to have found something to do. She hardly glanced at me.

"But, your shoes. You'll get your feet wet!" She didn't have boots, only her usual low shoes. And she'd complained to Daddy that the soles were so thin you could see through them. "Don't go, Mama."

"You're not afraid, are you?" Her voice held an edgy, hateful note. "I'll be back before dark. I'll bring you some candy."

I went to the back bedroom and came back just as she was pulling her collar up around her throat. "Here," I said. "Take this." I handed her the heavy green scarf Mrs. Meister had given me. "It'll keep you warm. Wrap it around your head."

Mama took the scarf. "Thanks, June. It'll help." She opened the door. "I've just got to get out of here."

I watched her figure, slim and black coated, disappear at the first curve in the road.

For two or three hours I kept busy: finished *Ivanhoe*, watched a fine snow swirling, and heated up the coffee from breakfast. It was bitter and strong, even with milk. Darkness encircled the house and me. The fire crackled as the wood burned and fell into ashes. The ticking of the clock sounded loud. There wasn't a sound outside unless I strained my ears. Faintly far over in a field beyond the new ground a cow bawled. A dog barked somewhere, its sharpness muted by the white stillness. I started reading out loud, playing for my own ears the parts of *Ivanhoe* and his love. I didn't want to read the bible or my school books. I pretended to read to PeeDee. She always liked to hear me read.

For supper I ate warmed up biscuits and butter mixed with molasses. I wasn't hungry enough to think about cooking anything. The woodpile, only a few yards from the back door, loomed white and large. I made sure the kitchen wood box was full, bringing in far more chunks of wood than I'd need, and I moved a stack to the outside wall of the house where snow wouldn't reach on the porch. I wondered about Mama. She must be at the neighbors' house. The Suttons were the closest. Beyond them, the Keevers lived a quarter of a mile or so before the highway. They'd likely convince her not to try walking back after dark.

I knew Mama wouldn't like it, but after I'd read myself hoarse and could hardly keep my eyes open, even worried as I was, I dragged my mattress off my bed and settled it in front of the kitchen stove. I stuffed towels under the kitchen door to keep the air out. The wind was not blowing hard, but sometimes it whistled around the house. I brought all the covers and slid under their weight. The clock said nine o'clock. I hoped Mama was as warm as I was.

The kitchen was much colder when I woke up, but lucky for me some coals still glowed and so I blew on my hands and clumsily placed kindling and paper to start the fire going. With the butt of a heavy knife, I broke the ice in the water bucket. Snow had drifted against the door so I used the slop jar. After putting the kettle on, I got back under the covers to wait for the kitchen to warm up. The fire in the front room had gone out. I lay there trying to decide what to do about breakfast. I had never made biscuits, but I thought I'd seen it done enough that I could do it.

When I woke up again, the fire needed more wood, but the water was good and hot. I poured coffee into the pot and waited. Then I made biscuits—and a mess. It had seemed so easy when Grandma mixed without measuring, slapped the dough on the floured surface of the table, rolled out the dough with the wooden rolling pin and with a twist of a jelly jar made neat circles of dough. I got them made and in the oven, but the kitchen was floury white and so were my clothes and shoes.

The world was totally quiet. I wished I had a dog to talk to, to pet, or even a cat. Mama said animals were too much trouble, what with our moving all the time, we couldn't be worrying about animals. I saw a picture of a cocker spaniel in a book and I thought that was the kind of dog I'd like. Nobody we knew had such a shiny, silky looking dog. If not a spaniel, maybe a little beagle pup. While the biscuits baked, I scrooched down under the covers again and a tear slid down my cold floury cheek. I picked up *Ivanhoe* and read some more.

Later in the morning, I took my mattress back to the bed. I didn't want Mama to get upset at seeing it out of place, and I cleaned up the kitchen as best I could. I wrapped one of the quilts around me and looked out the window, waiting to see a bird come out of hiding. I read my geography book, especially the part about the Tigris and Euphrates Rivers and tried to imagine palm trees and things like bull rushes from the Bible. I fed the fire and looked out the window. I imagined what everybody I knew was doing: Grandma and Grandpa and Johnnie would be in their front room, sewing, whittling, mending harnesses or something, and the quiet house would smell of apples or ham. All PeeDee's family would be together and even if Mr. Rednell was drinking, they would be talking and teasing. I knew they would. The Snyder girls were playing with their baby dolls. Daddy was somewhere. If he wasn't working, maybe he was resting for a change, just sitting and joking with some other men. Mama. She must be at a neighbor's house, maybe even worrying about me. Ivanhoe and his sweetheart were....

Daddy picked me up, quilt and all, and held me tight to his chest. His coat was damp and his hands gripping me even through the quilt were cold. "Baby, baby, thank God, you're all right."

"I'm okay, Daddy. I, I fell asleep." For a long moment, I felt secure, cocooned inside the quilt, bundled up. Daddy's eyes were red-rimmed and he hadn't shaved.

"Get us some coffee going, Alice, if there is any. Over there." I realized that two other people had come in behind Daddy. Mr. and Mrs. Keever. They stomped snow from their boots, and he peered into the front room stove.

"Where's Mama?"

"She won't be coming home for a few days, June." Daddy set me down and untangled the quilt from me. Already with three other people and the stoves being seen to, the house seemed warmer.

He squatted so we were almost eye level. I touched the stubble on his face, rough and reassuring. Daddy would shave as he did every morning and everything would be all right.

"You hungry?" He surveyed the kitchen. It still had plenty of signs that I'd made biscuits and some were in the warming oven. "Guess not, huh. I'm going to have one of these here biscuits myself."

He stood and took a biscuit. With some ceremony he bit into it, chewed and swallowed. "Good enough for company, I'd say, June." His eyes, red and tired as they were, had a tiny twinkle. He turned to the Keevers who were doing things around the stoves. "Here, my daughter's made us some biscuits, still warm."

Each of the Keevers took a biscuit, after wiping their hands on a dish towel. Daddy went into the front room for a minute.

Then he bent over me again, his hand on my hair. He held Mama's mirror before me. "You look like you've been to Sutton's grist mill," he said. He was grinning and he sounded proud of me.

"Where's Mama?" I asked again. "Did she get to the store? Is she coming home today?"

"She's staying at the Keevers for now, June. She'll be home in a few days, when she gets her strength back. Their oldest girl's looking after her now."

"We had to come see about you, June," Mrs. Keever said. She washed down the rest of the biscuit with a drink of water. "You managed, though, and are on your way to being a real biscuit baker."

I smiled at her. I trusted Mrs. Keever. She didn't say my biscuits were perfect. She didn't ever lie to me. I'd stopped at their house once or twice on my way home from school and once we'd gone to prayer meeting there.

"Well, what's wrong with Mama?"

I heard Mr. Keever mutter something that sounded like, "...darn fool, going out in this weather with a wet head, that's what." Mrs. Keever clattered the coffee pot on the stove.

"She's coming down with pneumonia, looks like." She measured the coffee. "The doctor can't come yet. But Betty's a good nurse, nursed her husband through his bad spell."

"One of the Keever boys found your mama in the road late last night."

In the front room, Mr. Keever muttered, "Coming home late as he was, out catting around till all hours..."

"It's a good thing, Albert, that young Al was out last night!" Mrs. Keever said.

"She was just about frozen to the ground," Daddy said. "Betty said if she hadn't had that scarf of yours wrapped around her head, she might've lost her ear."

"She'll be fine in a few days, June. Don't you worry." Mrs. Keever found coffee cups and put them before us. "I'm going to fry some streaked meat and eggs to go with these biscuits," she announced.

Daddy held me in my quilt on his lap while he sipped coffee. He rubbed his cheek. "Got to shave, huh, June?"

Things were getting back to normal. Mama was in a warm bed being looked after. Daddy was home. I looked up to see Mrs. Keever watching me eat. A thought occurred to me.

"Did Mama get me some candy at the store?"

In the silence, Daddy opened his mouth to say something. Mr. Keever said, "She got her some cigarettes, I know that."

Mrs. Keever said, "I declare, I believe I did see some candy in her coat pocket. I'll send one of the boys up here with it, June, soon as the snows melts a little."

I knew everything would be all right, but I wasn't sure I could believe Mrs. Keever from now on.

SPRINGTIME CAME A-GUSHING MISERY

Grandma's Passing

I SAW ONLY a faint glimmer of Grandma when I stood on tiptoes to peer into the casket. She looked like a doll, an old and gray doll, painted up ready to glide through the streets of gold. Except for that faint something that was herself. Her cheeks were fuller, plumper that they ever were and her expression was set and formal. Ready or not, she had to meet the public one last time.

DADDY HAD COME to the school to get me. When the principal came to the door and Mrs. Johnson beckoned me to the hallway, I knew it was bad news. But Grandma hadn't been sick, not that we knew of, and I couldn't believe what Daddy was saying. He told me as he led me down the dark hallway through the odor of oiled floors.

"No, she's not," I yelled and broke away from his hand. "No, she's not."

I ran into the sunlight of the school yard where Daddy caught me. He picked me up and I muffled my face in his shoulder.

"Yes, June. It happened last night. We just got word."

There was something strong and gruff in his voice, but something else, too. It sounded like he couldn't believe it either.

During the next days, Mama and Daddy were gone most of the time, and neighbor women came to stay with me. I wasn't to go back to school until after the funeral. Uncle Cade came and went, too. I asked a lot of questions, but nobody gave me any answers. Any answers that made sense. Grandma hadn't been sick, they said. "Well, what happened?" I wanted to know. "Seems like this spring's come a-gushing misery," one woman said.

"Don't go on with so many questions. You're a regular chatterbox," another neighbor said. I was left with a sense of confusion overlaid with trying to believe I wouldn't see Grandma in the summer, that there wouldn't be any more weeks at their house, that PeeDee wouldn't be visiting us.

We never did get up our courage to crawl under that gray rock cliff, but I liked thinking about it and we kept declaring we would do it before we got too big to get in and out of the space. Now it was like Grandma had herself slipped into a dark world, a mysterious under-the-cliff world. I dreamed of her under the cliff that first night and woke up mumbling and sweating.

Grandpa and Johnnie came by our house, but they didn't stay. Grandpa acted just the same. He said maybe twenty words the entire visit, and it seemed nobody had anything to say to him. Johnnie's eyes were red-rimmed and vague looking. Mama treated them like rank strangers, I thought, but she gave them coffee and warmed up leftovers so they could eat before going on home.

I caught Grandpa on the porch, while Mama and Daddy were still in the kitchen. "What was wrong with Grandma?"

Grandpa looked surprised that I would ask. He rubbed his stubbly face.

"She fell, hit her head." He squinted as if he could see over the hills if he tried hard enough.

I waited.

"Didn't come to."

I nodded and waited. He still squinted into the western sun, but he knew I was looking at him.

"Sent Johnnie for the doctor."

Daddy came out onto the porch, and Johnnie stood up. He'd been sitting on the steps, rubbing his shoe in the dust. "It was too late," Grandpa said.

"Too late," Johnnie mumbled.

The men walked toward the road. Mr. Alison was going to take them home, I guess, or somewhere.

WE WENT INTO the church where the coffin, open, had been placed at the front. There were some store bought wreaths, and Johnnie had brought bunches of holly with red berries to the church. Addie put the holly in some green vases and set them at the head of the coffin. She said that Johnnie wanted to put his mother's snuff can in the coffin with her. The preacher had said it was a heathenish thing to do and wouldn't allow it. I bet if anybody poked around in that coffin, they'd find Grandma's Dental Sweet snuff down at her side. If Johnnie wanted his mother to have it, he'd have found a time to slip it in the coffin. I couldn't connect the word "heathenish" up with putting a precious thing, her "nerve medicine" Grandma had called her snuff, in a casket. I know people were buried with their rings on and in their prettiest dresses, and some men who'd never in their life worn a necktie were buried in them.

We settled ourselves in on the front two or three rows, and the silence settled on us. It was broken by sniffles—colds or grief or both. After some twenty minutes or so of quiet, broken occasionally by muffled sobs and shaking shoulders, the group began, like an ice floe, to shift and mutter and break up at the edges. A child would shift places, someone would speak just above a whisper. A plump and pregnant wife moved to sit directly behind her husband, one of our cousins, and wrapped her arms around his neck.

The funeral director's voice was modulated to the occasion as he told us we might want a last viewing. They would be closing the casket in a few moments. Daddy, Johnnie, and his brother Jordon, stiff and straight in uniform, and his sister Evelyn made a final visit to the casket. Mama put her hand on my knee so I knew we wouldn't go by the casket again. Neither did Grandpa.

Then two men sort of glided down the aisle and, with some dignity and formality arranged the white quilted satiny material neatly, folding it inside the casket. with great care and slow movements. They lowered the lid and placed the large floral arrangement on the middle of the casket.

The piano player started with "The Old Rugged Cross." Then we sang "Softly and tenderly Jesus is calling, calling oh sinner come home, come home, come home." Untrained and unharmonious, our creaky, cracking, uneven, uncertain voices sounded as desolate as I'd heard that Coppertown, Tennessee, looked. I liked the next song: "In a land where we'll never grow old, never grow old, in a land where we'll never grow old." Grandma had been old as long as I'd known her, that's the way Grandmas were. I hoped Grandma found the streets of heaven level and smooth and not a bit steep.

I noticed Flo and her daughter Edwina. Flo's face was all crumpled, and Edwina was supporting her mother's sagging shoulders. Edwina wasn't more than thirty, but her long coarse black hair had big streaks of gray straying through it. She was crying silent tears, clutching a wadded-up handkerchief. Mama said she ran away from home with a wild boy who had stepped off the Trailways bus and just swooped her up and they left on the same bus. Mama said I wasn't to talk to her, that she'd given all five of her children away and that now she lived somewhere between Greenville and Atlanta. Wherever it was, it couldn't be "a land where we'd never grow old," because Edwina looked old already.

The preacher was younger than Preacher Duffey. He came down the left aisle and went to the raised up place so he stood above the casket. He wore a brown suit, loosely hanging on his frame; and he placed his Bible on the pulpit.

"I consider it an honor to be here today. It's an honor to be asked to help conduct the soul of this mother to the promised land. Mothers are wonderful people. We all ought to honor our mothers, and we do and these children and grandchildren do...."

Actually I was the only grandchild there, but I didn't think about that until later.

The preacher didn't talk much about Grandma. He didn't even know her. The regular preacher at Hamburg Baptist Church was in Florida. And this preacher said he was glad to have this pulpit to herd the unsaved toward the heavenly gates where we'd all have a chance to put stars in our crowns. He asked all those who had not "accepted the Lord Jesus as their Lord and savior" to see the Path of redemption, "the narrow way that leads to life everlasting, the only thing worth aiming for. Amen."

Finally, the preacher announced that he was glad that this mother had been saved, had accepted the lord Jesus. "And I tell you this, she didn't wait till a day before she went to meet Jesus in that great beyond, but I tell you this, brothers and sisters, she was ready. I thank God for this. Amen. She was ready as anybody on this old earth can be. Amen. She's gone to be with Jesus now. She don't have to suffer no more. She's not tied to that old body. She don't hurt anymore, Amen, and she'll be talking with the angels, Amen. There's no suffering in that great land beyond. Amen. There's no more suffering for them that's been saved. And I just hope and pray if they's any here today, Lord Jesus, who don't know the Lord as their savior, that you'll give your heart to the Lord, as she did. Amen."

He prayed a long time for our souls, with the hope that all who needed to would find the Lord so we could spend eternity with Grandma and all the other blessed souls who had entered into the kingdom of the Lord, where she'd "have a mansion, a mansion great and fair." Grandpa looked like he'd never be able to unclamp his jaw. Johnnie looked like he already inhabited another world. I couldn't see the expressions on Jordon and Evelyn. Anyway, they were just like rank strangers to me. I couldn't remember seeing them before and they never came back to see Daddy after the funeral. Mama fidgeted, while Daddy just stared straight ahead.

I tried to imagine Grandma in heaven, but she belonged to Bruton's Mountain, as strong-rooted as that old walnut tree near the spring. I just couldn't see her rejoicing in a white robe in a big mansion.

We sang "Farther along we'll know all about it, farther along we'll understand why." Then "No Tears in Heaven Fair, no tears no tears up there. All will be gladness in that land. No tears in heaven fair, no tears no tears up there..." The pallbearers (Robert and Ham and Mr. Watson, I recognized) came down the aisle and solemnly carried the casket toward the back. The preacher came down to shake hands with some while we followed the casket out.

The sunshiny day got all blurry and wavy, and I saw Grandma's casket being shoved under the gray rock cliff. I yanked my hand free and ran to save her. Daddy grabbed me from among the pallbearers' legs and carried me to the shade of the church. "Come on, June. You stay back here with Dr. Garret and his wife. They'll take you to their house and we'll come get you."

I must have been gasping for breath and crying at the same time. The Garrets came toward us. Daddy took something from his coat pocket. "Here, June. This is your Grandma's knife. You take it." He hugged me. "Every woman needs her own pocket knife. Maybe it'll be a comfort to you."

Mrs. Garret took my hand when he set me on the ground. "You be good, June. We'll pick you up in a little while." Daddy's shoulders shook as he turned to go bury his mama.

Grandpa's Going

I SAT ON THE hard wooden bench outside the door of the bleak room marked in gold letters on chicken-wire glass "Sheriff's Office." The hall of the courthouse was bare, except for a few benches. Mama and Daddy were talking to Uncle Cade and had been in there a long time. I didn't know why we were at the courthouse. Daddy told me we'd see Grandpa before he had to go to a big hospital in Burke County.

Things after Grandma's funeral were blurry for me. I didn't remember being taken home after Grandma's funeral. For days I had lain in a darkened room and was even visited by Dr. Garret.

I remember hearing Daddy's low, coarse whisper: "She's not getting better. I'm going for the doctor."

Mama replied, "It's just chicken pox, for goodness' sake, Carl. Every kid gets the chicken pox."

Daddy's voice had dropped lower, "It's that and Ma's dying like she did."

He put on his hat and went for the doctor who poked and looked down my throat and at my itchy face and thumped my chest. The doctor didn't look too worried, but I heard snatches of talk as he downed a cup of coffee in the kitchen. "Rheumatic fever's going around. Keep her warm. Give her these. Let her sleep all she can. Send for me if there's any change for the worse."

I YAWNED WIDELY and quickly covered my mouth like a lady. Lately, Mama kept telling me to act like a lady. I held my little red purse tightly. Aunt Mattie had brought me the purse and she'd put some nickels in it, too. My feet barely touched the floor and my legs ached. I was tired and foggy all over. I doubled my body into a curl on the bench and almost slept.

The door opened and Daddy said, "Well, Cade, it's a sorry business all right. But there ain't no help for it now. We got to do what we got to do." Daddy had sun wrinkles around his eyes and worry lines in his face.

"Of course." The sheriff stepped aside so Mama could come out into the hallway, and he locked the office door. "Well, look at that," he said. I pretended to sleep, not wanting to irritate Mama.

"It's not been easy, hauling June around settling this," Mama said. "She's big enough to stay home by herself."

My daddy picked me up. "She's been sick. She doesn't know what's going on," he said.

"You all want to go over to the hospital, I reckon, before dinner and finish signing the papers?" Uncle Cade said.

"Let's get it over with," Mama said. Uncle Cade was her half-brother, from her daddy's first family before he moved to Clayton, Georgia, but they didn't act like it mattered at all.

"Have you seen Pa today?" Daddy asked.

Sheriff Cade nodded. One gold tooth to the left of center marred his smile. "He was calm, friendly. Asked about the family, asked about your mama. Of course he called her 'Woman'."

Daddy's face burned. "That damn fool. He keeps on with this pretending. He knows Ma is dead! He knows well enough."

"Don't start, Carl," Mama said. "Don't say that. He's gone completely."

Daddy's jaw muscles tensed. "He don't know, I guess. If he did we wouldn't be doing this now. It be would be clear-cut...if he remembered that day..."

"Your ma's been dead more than three weeks now, and he doesn't recollect the death or the funeral," Mama reminded him. She impatiently applied lipstick and snapped her purse shut.

"No, and he don't know she was killed by a lick on the head either," Daddy muttered.

The sheriff said sternly, "Carl, the coroner's report and the inquest showed that the death could have been caused by a fall against a hard sharp object." He frowned. "Ain't right to keep accusing your pa of downright murder, not without evidence."

Mama clutched Daddy's arm, wanting to hurry him out of there. Holding me carefully, he put his free arm awkwardly around her waist.

"It's been awful hard on Rose—keeping Pa these last weeks. Always worrying. He's not happy at our house. Sometimes he's a-raving, sometimes quiet and deadly like a cocked shotgun."

"At least Johnnie's out of it, down at your sister's," Uncle Cade said.

At the County Hospital, Daddy placed me on Mama's lap, but I was heavy and she moved me to the bench and smoothed her dress. Daddy paced up and down the black-checkered floor. Smoking nervously, he reminded me of one of Grandpa's hounds penned up during hunting season. Finally Sheriff Cade said in his slow way, "It's not an easy thing for a man to do, Bruton."

"It's the only thing he can do," Mama said quickly.

"Looks like the only thing." The sheriff nodded.

Old Dr. Garret entered the room. He spoke briefly to their greetings. His eyes were sad.

"You want to get on with it?" he asked gruffly.

Daddy nodded. "How is he?"

"Calm. Not giving anybody any trouble. Completely happy in his own fashion."

"Happy?" Mama almost sneered.

"He's unaware of his surroundings, Rose."

"Oh. Will he know us?"

"Maybe. If you want to see him. Here are the necessary papers of commitment. Sign here and on the next two pages." The doctor pushed the papers toward Daddy who stood woodenly at the table's edge. He glanced at Mama, at the sheriff, at the doctor. He looked down at the papers.

"Doc," he said, "if there is any chance, I mean, is there any help for him down there? Or here?"

"My son, that's up to a higher power than myself to say. At the moment it seems almost hopeless." The doctor shrugged. "The way he gets sometimes, you know you can't—and the hospital can't keep him here."

"And the jail can't keep him," Uncle Cade said.

Daddy stood rigid, the pen poised, awkward-looking, in his hand. Then he burst out, "Oh my God! I know he done it! I know it." He scribbled on the papers before him. Perspiration dampened his upper lip. The room was silent. I heard the traffic down the hill, and far off, some crazy rooster crowed at this time of day.

"I'll have him brought out here for a few minutes," the doctor said. "Then Cade, you can take him."

Everybody nodded. Daddy sank into a chair when the doctor left. I wanted to cry. When the door opened with a click a few moments later, he jumped up.

Grandpa wore clean pressed black pants and a white shirt. There was a tiny blob of blood on his scrubbed and clean shaven face. An orderly stood outside the open door.

"Pa," said Daddy.

Grandpa said in a sing-song voice, "The wagons are a-coming again. I hear them chains away down the road."

"He thinks somebody is going to pick him up in a wagon. Been hearing chains all day and last night," the orderly said.

I walked over to Grandpa. He looked like he knew me, but not quite. He patted my head like I was old Lash. He'd never done that before. "Bye, June, you be a good girl now," he said. "They're getting closer. Them chains are a-creaking."

He looked around at the walls that closed us in. "Ah, Lord, reckon I'm going to a better place."

Mama pulled me away and yanked me out the door. I saw tears in Daddy's eyes as Uncle Cade led Grandpa down the hall toward a waiting car. He was declaring, "They're getting closer. Them chains a-getting closer."

Backsliding and Baptizing

THE TUCKASEEGEE RUNS deep in some places, shallow in others, shadowed by trees, dappled by sunlight, twisting and then smooth and straight. "Like life," the preacher said. "That old river's like life itself."

At one point, down from Piney Fork Church, an island intruded itself in the flow, and a part of the river wandered around it, creating a natural spot for baptisms. The water was deep enough, no deeper than a man's waist and shallower near the bank. Over the years a path had been worn down to the river from the road that runs above it. Considering how many baptisms had occurred there, the number of feet that had trod the path, it was still very narrow.

As the rains wore it down, the path became a natural gully to the river and a natural metaphor for the preachers thereabouts. "Life, brothers and sisters, is like that track down to the river, down to the Lord's watering hole. It's narrow and it's not easy to stay on it, but it's worth it, Lord, to get to the blessed house of the lord. Heaven don't come at the end of no wide and easy road, no sir, it don't. You got to want to get there and you got to stay on the Lord's way--narrow and hard as it is."

The Lord's way being narrow as it was, some people fell by the wayside. Backsliding it was called. Backsliding was a way of life for Les Bob Sutton. Some folks said he kept the preachers in business. If Les had not backslid enough to get re-converted, well, it had not been a very exciting year.

I'd gone to the revival with Aunt Mattie. Les staggered down the aisle. He wasn't drunk, not on revival days, just loose jointed, always just about ready to fly into pieces. All his appendages flopped and ambled. It was a miracle he got down to the altar without following his wandering arms and knees in the direction of first one side of the church, then the other.

He made it and fell to his knees before Preacher Duffey. On either side were four other sinners who had responded to the call, new to the conversion experience. Not like Les. He was a regular. Every revival meeting. And for good reason. His exploits kept the community entertained. He wasn't really bad, but he tended to get caught. He liked the food at the jail and could count on Mrs. Orton fixing him cobbler every time. That's because he was so charming. He could charm the birds right off their nests, women said.

"Lord, I have sinned and come up short. I aim to do right. I've give my life to you, Lord, before and I'm here again. A sinner. Lord, forgive me." He bowed his head, his hands clasped in prayer.

Preacher Duffey put both hands on Les's shoulders. His voice was lower and I couldn't hear all he said, but it went something like this: "Brother, are you truly repentant? Are you giving your true self, your soul and yourself to God? Are you ready to accept him as your savior? Pray about it, brother. This is not a decision to make lightly nor to scoff at. Are you willing to change your ways, ready to accept the Lord's burden? Can you give up the ways of the world and dedicate your life to him, to the Lord who died on the cross for you, brother, for the sweet Jesus who died on the cross for all of us sinners in this room. The sinners here at the altar and the sinners on the benches. We're all sinners and we need the grace of the Lord."

Tears rolled down Les's face, stalling in his full mustache, sliding into the corners of his mouth. His loose body was steady as if it were held in place with bailing wire. Then he shook all over. He lowered his head even further, his forehead touching the floor where Preacher Duffey stood, one step higher than the converts. He nodded, almost banging his head on the floor. "I'm ready, Preacher. I hear what you're saying. I know I'm a sinner and I know there's grace abounding for all who love the Lord."

Preacher Duffey asked the others at the front to kneel while he led us in prayer. He asked the congregation to get off the benches and onto their knees before the Lord, too. Some people had already moved to the aisle to kneel; others slipped down in front of the pews. Some of us sat with heads down and eyes mostly closed. I'd seen Les's rededication a couple of times before. I hope Preacher Duffey believed him. And the Lord, of course. I know I did.

After the final hymn, people went up to shake hands with the new and rededicated Christians and to welcome them to the church's bosom. A baptizing in a few weeks would make their commitments definite. As I filed up, gently guided by Aunt Mattie, and shook Les's hand, I tried to remember where I'd seen him last. It came to me: at his baptizing last year. After the dipping in the Tuckaseegee River we'd all gone up to Deacon Alison's house so the baptized could dry off and change clothes and have fellowship and eat cake and drink coffee. I'd gone around the corner of the house to see the new litter of kittens. Les was dripping wet and he had his hand on Evelyn Jones' equally dripping wet breast.

Just about everybody I knew got baptized at one time or another, and some more than once. Except Mr. Rednell. He didn't darken a church door. People seemed determined to backslide, though, and equally joyful to rejoin the ranks of the saved after months or years of their hell-bent sinful conditions. So, every year enough people gathered for baptism to make it a festive occasion.

I knew that one day I'd be more than an on-looker, but the spirit hadn't touched me yet, even though I was approaching the "age of decision" and the congregation would be eying me closely at every altar call, especially at revivals.

PeeDee resisted going to church and wouldn't talk about it. Her lips got tight when I mentioned it. She didn't scoff, but she held back from saying something, I could tell. Her older brothers had been baptized, and her mother was among the nine people who would enter the fold this Sunday afternoon. I didn't understand why PeeDee wouldn't even come when her own mother was going to be baptized.

Mrs. Rednell had been almost carried to the altar, supported by the arms of Mamie Alison and the preacher. Behind me a woman whispered, "Poor thing. She looks poorly as death eating a cracker."

Mrs. Rednell had started trembling and shaking and moaning to herself, and she allowed the two to walk her to the front of the church. She kept asking forgiveness and saying, "Lord, I don't know what to do, Lord help me, Lord, tell me what to do," and on and on like that. The revival preacher prayed over her, and Preacher Duffey assured her of the Lord's blessings. She quieted down as he clamped on her head and

134

asked the Lord's help in vanquishing the demons of "this poor woman."

She whimpered and nodded when he asked her if she was sure of her decision, did she commit her life into the hands of the Lord. She seemed to give an inward shiver, sort of cave in, and then make all the right responses. Without thinking about it, I felt that she had given up something at that very moment: sin, responsibility, hope, or something.

The day was warm, a perfect day for immersion. The water would be cold, cold as always, but sunshine in early April was taken as a good omen. "A good day for baptizing," the preacher said. "The Lord's seen fit to bless this day and these good people who are joining his kingdom in the sunshine of his blessings."

We straggled down the recently graveled road. I counted at least twenty-five people. Most went directly down the path to the level shoreline where they stood talking or just waiting; others stopped in at the Alison house, almost directly above the baptizing place, on the bank above the road which snaked above the river. Afterwards, those baptized and baptizing always went, along with their families, friends, well-wishers, and church officials, up to the Alison house. The afternoon was a long lingering time after the main event.

We joined in the singing of "Shall we gather at the river" and followed it by "There's power in the blood, power in the blood," and "Just As I am, without one plea." Deacon Deuce Alison got us started with a little instrument he put to his lips to indicate "pitch." I thought that meant that after that pause for the sound, we all pitched in and sang. But Aunt Mattie corrected me. "That gives us the right note to start on, so we all sound in harmony." I don't think it exactly worked.

Preacher Duffey asked for Pinky Shears to come forth. I thought he'd dignify the occasion by giving Pinky his birth certificate name, Comstock, but he called right out, "Pinky, come on down. The Lord's ready to put his seal on you." Of course, Pinky probably hardly remembered his real name by now. He was over fifty, never married, pink-faced, and lumbering. His granddad, who had gone out west as a young man, had given him the fanciful name of Comstock. Comstock didn't even make it through the first year. And Pinky had been Pinky ever since.

He, like the other men to be baptized, wore dark pants and white shirts, their Sunday clothes. Pinky knew the routine; he'd been immersed twice before. Whatever his failures, he was generally a respected member of the church. Some said he visited a loose woman in Macon County too often, maybe even had a whole family over there. But his face was so innocent, his eyes so untroubled blue, his thinning hair so neat that I couldn't believe anything of him except that he worked at the train depot ("Free transportation to Macon," people said.) and kept a tobacco allotment.

The Preacher began the ceremony with various scriptures: "We're one in the body of the Lord and we got one hope: One Lord, one faith, one baptism in the faith. Brothers and sisters, we're gathered here to wash away the sins of our fellow men, just as Christ died to wash away our sins with his blood. He don't ask our blood, brothers and sisters, but he does ask us to show ourselves willing, to come down before Him and his people and wash out the impurities. These people have repented before us all, like Peter said, Repent and ye shall be saved..."

PeeDee's mother was the first woman that day to enter the water. For some reason men always went first in the baptizings, at least at Preacher Duffey's baptizings. Her name was Cora, Corie to most people, and she was pale and gaunt. I saw her mostly at church or funerals because Mr. Rednell didn't particularly like visitors and he kept his family close to home.

I could see a little of PeeDee in Mrs. Rednell's broad forehead and blondish hair. But PeeDee was already as tall as her mother, and she'd look directly at you and not be stared down by teacher or bully or bigger girl. Mrs. Rednell was hesitant. Her eyes flickered toward Preacher Duffey who led her into the deeper water and then off toward the other bank of the river. This was a big step she was taking, her first real baptism, folks said. She'd told Mrs. Alison she'd been baptized way back when she was young in the Methodist Church in the Piedmont, but that didn't count. She'd just been sprinkled then. Corie's name, said Mrs. Alison, might be on the rolls of that faraway church, but she needed to make her peace with her Lord here and so she had. Except she didn't look at peace.

Aunt Mattie said, "Something's troubling that woman. If she's expecting the Lord to deal with it..."

She noticed me listening and said, "Little pitchers have big ears, don't they? Pay me no never-mind."

"Well, everybody knows Mr. Rednell drinks."

"And has all their married life and before, I reckon. That's not new. No, that's not it." Aunt Mattie wiped her forehead. "I'm beginning to think like Cade, I reckon. Don't listen to me."

The preacher prayed over Mrs. Rednell, and he and the deacon placed a hand under her elbow and the deacon put his left hand at the small of her back and they lowered her into the water. It was a most graceful immersion. She didn't come up sputtering like some did. She went directly to the deacon's wife who wrapped a big cotton cloth around her to preserve her dignity and hide any curves of her body that might draw more than religious thoughts.

Friends and family waited to embrace each person who waded to the bank a "different creature now, a God-forgiven Christian." Even Aunt Mattie hugged Mrs. Rednell and we straggled back up the path to the deacon's house.

My head was full of thoughts that ought not to have been there. Was baptizing a washing of the dirt away from the soul like washing your hands? Just living got your hands dirty all over again. Did your soul just routinely get dirty? How did you know when the time was right to deliver your soul to God for cleansing?

I guess I'd know when the time was right. Maybe you didn't recognize the dirt until it accumulated and weighed you down. People talked about the weight of sin, of sin and doubt, of the heavy load they carried. Clearly the baptizing brought joy to the new and renewed Christians. They laughed and cried happy tears. They shook hands and joined the fellowship of the saved. Baptizings were happy occasions. But I left that afternoon, with a backward look at Mrs. Rednell, pale and eyes downcast, tagging behind Aunt Mattie, with a sense of confusion, even sadness.

LATE APRIL 1945

Schoolyard Fray before the Funeral

"YOUR MAMA DON'T love you!" Louellen's hissed words hit me with hurricane force. We were playing at the edge of the school ground, various groups of us creating our little kingdoms, drawing our houses in the dirt, arranging sticks and rocks and generally playacting.

Aunt Mattie had kept me at home with her the day after Uncle Cade was shot, but on Wednesday, even before the funeral, she sent me to school. I felt like a piece of cold, glazed, hardened taffy. PeeDee and I stuck close together, not talking. Her daddy was in jail, my uncle was dead because of him, and Mama and Daddy had left me. Didn't seem to be much to say.

But I was trying to act normal, like Aunt Mattie instructed, "Just act normal, June. Things will be all right." So I stepped into the square that Louellen had drawn as her house. Right then she took her foot and erased our fort's edge. I picked up the old broom someone had found down by Scott's Creek and wiped out her roof line.

Something about Louellen always irritated me. It might have been her absolutely beautiful curls, shining clean and long. She'd never had her hair cut as long as she lived. Sometimes I called her curls frizzy, but she didn't take offense at that. She knew she was cute as a button, and her curls were her glory. And they weren't really frizzy. I envied those curls, me with my straight brown hair. Anyway, today I was mad at the world even if I was acting normal.

I accidently on purpose swept her doll out of her house. Louellen had so many dolls she could risk bringing one to school. But she didn't want this one swept around. PeeDee laughed. Louellen kicked at me and then she butted me in the stomach. That surprised me. She was usually more lady like. I pushed her, but not hard. Her daddy owned Snyder's Store across on the main street, and sometimes he handed out candy. I was partial to Mary Janes, those little peanut butter blocks. I didn't want to hurt Louellen or hurt my chances of free candy.

The other girls started paying attention as we pushed and picked at each other. She called me "a meanie" and I called her "prissy."

"Smart alec, smarty pants, "she yelled.

"Miss frizzhead," I yelled back.

She butted at me again and my elbow hit her nose, her cute little turned up nose. Bright blood dripped all down her checked blue jumper and white blouse. Louellen burst into tears. She just plunked down and started bawling. Her older sister, who was thirteen, had been playing with the bigger girls. I didn't see her coming. Louanne grabbed me behind and shook me. That's when Louellen stopped crying and hissed out her words.

"She never did want you. Your mama don't love you!"

The brownish yellow leaves blurred. "You're lying!"

I couldn't get to Louellen. She'd scooted backwards into the protective circle of her friends. So I punched at Louanne who grabbed my corduroy overall straps. Louanne hauled off and smacked me hard. What had blurred in shame and fury now turned to stars and blackness. My lip bled. Louanne yanked me up and started shaking me hard. My teeth rattled. My bubble gum popped out of my mouth and landed in the dirt. She outweighed me by twenty pounds at least.

She outweighed PeeDee too. But PeeDee jumped on her back and got her in a stranglehold. Louanne started going in circles, trying to dislodge PeeDee, smacking her as best she could with one hand, trying to pry PeeDee's arm from around her neck with the other. Louanne stumbled close to me and I stuck my foot out. She went down, PeeDee still hanging on.

Louanne looked purple, like she was going to pass out. PeeDee looked like Annie Oakley on a wild bronco.

Mr. Clontz shouted, "That's enough. Stop it, girls." He and Mrs. Sherrill and Miss Johnson pried PeeDee off Louanne. We were all a sorry sight. Louellen's tears and nosebleed had ruined her face and her clothes. My lip was puffed up. But Louanne was downright sick. She threw up right in front of all of us.

Louellen and Louanne went home. They lived close to the school. PeeDee and I went to the principal's office.

"She does, she did want me," I said. "What does Louellen know!"

Miss Johnson wiped dirt from my face and dabbed Mercurochrome on my cut lip. "Of course, honey. Don't pay any attention to her."

"Did you start it?" The principal looked at PeeDee, slumped in a chair, her fist under her chin. "At a time like this—" He stopped and chewed on a pencil. PeeDee wasn't his favorite pupil. For one thing, she missed a lot of school and for another, she didn't try to look repentant. Anybody knew if a girl looked remorseful and cried a little, Mr. Clontz would believe anything.

"She didn't start it," I spoke up.

"Well, somebody did," the principal said.

"I started it, I guess. Louellen messed up my house and I,I started it."

Mr. Clontz didn't seem convinced. PeeDee didn't seem interested in joining in.

"If you started it, June, I'll have to punish you..."

"Mr. Clontz," Miss Johnson stopped dabbing at me, "don't you think..."

"Don't you do anything to her," PeeDee said fiercely. "That bitch didn't have the right to say that."

"Punish you," Mr. Clontz repeated. "We can't condone fighting on the playground, Miss Johnson, regardless of the circumstances."

He turned to me. "I don't think paddling will help in this case. You'll have to stay after school the rest of the month, starting after the funeral, of course. Miss Johnson, set her to writing on the board. Whatever you think is appropriate." He looked weary. "And you, Prudence, I'm going to ignore your language this time. I don't want to hear that word from you again. Is that clear?"

PeeDee nodded. Her face was smudged and her pigtails were a mess. But to me she was Annie Oakley winning rodeos all over the west.

Miss Johnson put away her medicine kit. "You girls stay away from the Snyder girls for awhile. And," she said, "I think you should apologize to them."

PeeDee started to say something and I opened my mouth to protest. Miss Johnson winked. "After all, they came off the worst in the fray."

Fray. I liked that word. Fray. Sounded better than fight. Maybe boys fight and girls fray. Anyway, I stayed after school the rest of the month and wrote on the board one hundred times every day for a week: "I will be nice. I will not fight." Miss Johnson wouldn't let me write "I will not fray." And being an English teacher, she had to explain the difference. I listened carefully, but it stood to reason that if "fight" could be a noun and a verb, "fray" ought to have the same privilege. She further explained that English doesn't necessarily stand to reason. "Just," she said gently, "as it doesn't stand to reason for you not to apologize."

I thought about it, and after school the next week as Louellen and Louanne crossed the bridge connecting the school ground and the town, I caught up with them.

"I have to go back and write on the board," I said, "but will you please accept my apology for the other day?" I had practiced that. "I'm sorry, and PeeDee is too."

PeeDee had said she wasn't and she wouldn't apologize, but she wouldn't mind if I lied a little white lie.

Louanne frowned, but Louellen said, "We forgive you. I'm sorry I said that about your mother. I didn't mean it."

I figured we were even. We'd both told our white lies. Still I didn't know if Mr. Snyder would ever offer me another free Mary Jane.

Uncle Cade's Funeral Day

"I'M RIGHT SORRY about your uncle," PeeDee told me.

We stood at the edge of the graveyard, waiting for the grownups to wander away from the grave. PeeDee couldn't know that when tears had found their way from my insides to out, in the dark of the nights between the day of the news and the funeral, they had been more for me and for her than for Uncle Cade. Now, my eyes were frozen ponds. A tear couldn't have escaped any more than a leaf caught in the ice all winter.

I was now "Mattie's girl," in the community view. It was like my mama and daddy had been wiped out or like they'd just been passing through the county, not permanent folks. They just drove away, suitcases in hand. And left me.

As I helped around the edges during the funeral days, I heard people say, "Ask Mattie's girl to fetch us some clean plates," or "Mattie's girl's growing up, ain't she." Like I'd been lent to my parents and they had returned me, to fill a void, now doubly deep in Aunt Mattie's house. Surely people talked about my new status. Surely someone asked why, where, how, but I didn't hear a thing.

Scraps of overheard tidbits told me Mama and Daddy had left the borrowed car and caught the Grayhound bus out of Sylva, headed for Washington. "Didn't buy a round trip ticket according to that Maggie who works there."

During the funeral days, people spoke and smiled and ignored me. A few touched my shoulder briefly maybe in a gesture of sympathy. Mrs. Hall even pulled me to her lap and said, "You'll be all right, child, you'll be fine here." Then she seemed embarrassed and stood up, losing her lap. She didn't catch my eye again.

I did all I could to help Aunt Mattie. I dusted off her Sunday shoes. I got out the bottle of black shoe polish to brighten them up. I never let the water bucket go empty or the wood box. Others also did a lot of fetching and carrying. Everybody wanted to spare Aunt Mattie. With losing her boy Nyle and now her husband, she'd suffered more than a person had a right to expect, and I knew it wasn't my place to make her suffer more.

The church house was full for the funeral, and a lot of people couldn't get inside. I didn't pay a lot of attention to the preacher because Aunt Mattie squeezed my hand so hard I concentrated on that. At the graveyard PeeDee must have felt kind of awkward. She'd come with her mother and some neighbors and they stood outside, quite a ways outside, the funeral tent at the graveyard. Her father was in jail but not yet charged with the murder of Uncle Cade. Nobody was charged yet. The family wasn't talking. Old Man Rednell said over and over he didn't fire the shot that killed the sheriff. There had not been a struggle, no bruises on the body. None of the kids had actually seen, they said, what happened. It was as if a shot had simply occurred, unwitnessed.

Uncle Cade died, they said, with his gun still in his holster. Somebody would have to be charged, but it boiled down to no reliable witnesses. In fact, no witnesses who could say anything with certainty. Mrs. Rednell swore she'd gone to the kitchen, to stir the stewed potatoes. She'd locked the front door against Mr. Rednell and he was kicking at the screen door. Marvin had been at the outer circle of the yard. The girls had been hiding in the house when the shot was fired and when they ran to the front room, it was over.

PeeDee and her brothers could only say that the sheriff had arrived; they'd heard that. Benjy had immediately gone to the outhouse after having more or less delivered the sheriff. He and Marvin had hurried to find the doctor and other lawmen when they saw Uncle Cade in the yard, blood beginning to ooze from beneath his body. All this I fit together from the men who clustered outside the house and outside the funeral home. PeeDee's father swore he didn't do it, but he'd been drunk, that was sure, and the pistol was his. Apparently just about every Rednell had picked up that pistol, and apparently somebody had wiped it fairly clean.

"What will you all do?" I asked.

PeeDee shrugged. "Make do, I guess."

She looked at the people filtering our way. "Mama's coming. I can't stay. People will talk about us coming at all. But, but," she faltered just a little, "June, I hate you have to live with your aunt Mattie."

It was my turn to shrug. "It's okay. Guess I'll see you at school Monday."

"No, didn't you know? Mama's taking us all to her family for the rest of the school year. Marvin can work in the cotton mills. He's old enough. Me, I'll probably be put back another grade." She turned to look toward the east. She seemed thinner and taller than just the week before. Her hand clenched a handkerchief and her fingernails were bitten down to the quick.

Her words melted the ice in my soul and tears rolled down my face. I quickly wiped my sleeve across my face. PeeDee leaving. PeeDee gone. My mind kept shouting no, it's not true, but my tears plopping on the dusty ground told me I believed it.

"Can't you stay here? You could stay with us—with Aunt Mattie and me."

She didn't turn around. "No, you know I can't do that. They're letting us go, but Daddy can't. He can't leave the county. People are getting sort of mean and hateful to us." She sounded remote, almost grown up.

"PeeDee, I'll write. I'll write every single week." I wiped my nose, smearing the sleeve of my best dress. My voice wasn't steady, but I willed my tears to stop. I didn't want everybody to see me crying. "Will you write to me?"

"I'm not much for writing," she muttered. That was true. PeeDee was one for doing. I could do the writing for both of us.

"Here," PeeDee said. "I want you to keep this to remember me by."

She brought from her pocket a tiny locket, no bigger than a man's thumbnail. It was her dearest possession. If I hadn't known how much she treasured it, I would have envied it.

It was just a matter of luck that she had the locket, not me. One day we'd been walking home from school, just the two of us, ahead of the others. Some convicts were working on the road that day, cutting brush and digging culverts. Two heavy set men with rifles guarded them. The convicts had leg chains on. One of the guards motioned us to cross over and walk on the other side of the highway and we did. The men looked up, swung their tools more tentatively. I'd heard about prisoners working on the chain gang, but this was the first time I'd ever seen men in striped prison clothes, and I guess I stared. One of the prisoners threw up a hand at us and I waved right back.

"Hey, little girls," the man called out. His voice was really soft.

"Hey," we said. We kept walking, but more slowly.
"What's your name, little Miss?" another man said.

PeeDee didn't answer, so I said, "I'm June and this is Prudence Delilah." It didn't seem right, somehow, to call her PeeDee to them. This was a formal occasion.

The guard stood still as a squinty-eyed rock, both hands on his rifle. But he didn't say to quit talking.

"Hey, Ralph," one man said to the guard, "this'un reminds me of my little Katie, about the same age."

He put down his shovel and slowly put his hand in his pocket. He pulled out a nickel. "Here, little'un. Buy yourself a popsicle." He flipped the nickel with complete accuracy across the highway and I caught it in the air.

"Thanks, mister," I said. The nickel had an Indian head on it. "I don't have anything to give you back."

"Just enjoy a popsicle on me." He winked. "Banana's my favorite."

"Mine, too. Thanks a lot."

We'd stopped walking and the guard motioned us to keep moving. PeeDee looked completely forlorn. Maybe because one of her cousins, she'd told me, was working on the road down in Florida. Anyway, she looked mighty sad, especially as she admired my shiny nickel.

Another prisoner leaned on his shovel. He took something from his shirt pocket and threw it across the road. "A pretty girl like you deserves a pretty trinket," he said.

It was the silver locket. His action caught us by surprise, and the locket landed in the dirt at PeeDee's feet. She grabbed it and her face lit up. And the man's face did, too. She stared at it and started to put it around her neck, then noticed the clasp was broken. So as not to embarrass the giver, she just held it up to her chest and grinned at him. She thanked him and asked him his name. He didn't answer.

"Move on, girls," the guard Ralph said. "Get on, now."

We waved and skipped on, stopping to look back several times. The guards must have told the prisoners to keep working. They weren't looking at us.

THAT PIECE OF jewelry was the first one PeeDee owned, and now it could be my first one.

"I can't take it, PeeDee. You love it more'n this world, you know you do."

"What am I going to do with this old locket down in the Piedmont?" She had used white thread to secure the two ends of the locket. Now she put it over my neck. Her rough fingernail scratched the nape of my neck. "Likely I'll get me a boyfriend down there who'll buy me a new locket, anyway."

"A boyfriend?"

"I'm old enough for a boyfriend. A real boyfriend, not like Jamie and Leon. They're silly."

I couldn't fathom why she had boyfriends on her mind at this minute. The locket was cool on my neck, but it didn't seem right to take it. Nothing seemed right. I couldn't imagine not having PeeDee as my best friend, couldn't imagine her in some flat place, some flat place that might have snow, but not much. My views of the Piedmont were gleaned mostly from the newspapers on the wall of Annie and Robert's house. I didn't think I'd like it.

"Come on, Prudence Delilah. Say goodbye to June and come on." PeeDee's mother didn't stop to speak to me. She walked quickly, her head down and her shoulders hunched up.

"I have to go, June." PeeDee wasn't about to hug me and I felt like my feet had grown roots and couldn't move. "Bye." She looked at the locket again and at me. Her lips quivered just a little.

"I'll write you, PeeDee, I'll write every chance I get. Maybe you can come back pretty soon. Maybe it'll be awful down there. And listen, I don't care, I don't really care if your Daddy did it. I mean, it's not like it was you or something. I mean, I'm sorry Uncle Cade is dead, but I don't blame you. I hope your Daddy don't get..."

I was chattering, like I never did. I wanted to hold on to PeeDee, to hug her. I didn't want her to go off and leave me. Everybody was leaving me. She ducked her head, sort of like her mother, and said again, "Bye, June."

GROWING UP FOR SURE

Getting By

AUNT MATTIE DIDN'T talk much about Uncle Cade after the funeral. She kept her grief inside, like a chipmunk can burrow deep inside the frigid winter earth and leave no visible trace outside. And she didn't eat much, just got thinner than ever and her dresses already hung loosely on her big-boned frame. But she had never been one to chatter.

After Nyle's death she had retreated completely for months. Now she glided through her everyday chores with hardly a sound. In the kitchen, Mama had often been loud and clangy, dropping pan lids and clattering dishes, but Aunt Mattie put food on the table with efficiency and silence. She kept us both busy, scrubbing, dusting, cleaning out dresser drawers and washing every quilt in the house.

After a few weeks, she sent for the preacher and loaded him down with Uncle Cade's clothes and boots. She told him to give them to anybody that needed them. People said it was good that the preacher took them all over to Yancey County where he had cousins and uncles the right size. That way she wouldn't see a familiar shirt on somebody in town.

I never asked if she missed Uncle Cade and she never asked if I missed Mama and Daddy. Words were a commodity we didn't waste. Once I asked about Grandpa and Johnnie, and Aunt Mattie said they were being taken care of, Grandpa in a big brick building, Johnnie in his sister's "cotton mill house." That I couldn't imagine. But I imagined Mama at the ocean, walking in warm white sand, picking up sand dollars by the dozen. I imagined Daddy smiling at her in the sunshine and her smiling back. Nobody ever said a word about our furniture. Maybe they had sold it. Anyway I had everything I owned with me, and now more than I had brought. A new scratchy wool dress for the funeral, one reserved for Sunday and church, a few books that Aunt Mattie's town friends brought to me, Grandma's knife, and the locket PeeDee gave me.

For a long time I tried to hurry Aunt Mattie when we went to the post office to see if we had mail. One day she cautioned me, "Don't get your hopes up, June." And I slowed down to walk beside her. We didn't get much mail, one or two official looking letters, "from the government." One day, though, Aunt Mattie got a postcard from Evelyn, Daddy's sister in the Piedmont. It said that Johnnie was okay, in a special school, and that Leonie was in Las Vegas, married to a casino man. "I hope that poor girl gets on with her life," Aunt Mattie remarked and then she tried to explain what a casino man did for a living.

Aunt Mattie didn't want to hear me go on about PeeDee. A glint of hardness came into her eyes when I mentioned my friend or her family. She simply would not engage in any talk about them beyond a lip-tightened "Hmm" or a semi-grunt. One day we were both in the kitchen. I was just watching her churn. In the silence, I sometimes wondered things out loud. "Louanne said they have oleo, not real butter in the Piedmont," I said. "I bet PeeDee's missing this kind of butter."

"The farther away that family is, the better. Always into some devilment and it come down to death at last." The harshness in her tone surprised me.

"PeeDee's not a bad girl—" I started to protest.

"Let's hear no more about them, June. Your uncle's dead because of somebody in that family and it looks like they're going to go scot free." She looked up from her chore. "Take that pot from the stove."

The pumpkin had been simmering for pies. I placed the heavy pot beside the sink.

"Well..." I started again, but I stopped.

"Good riddance, girl." Aunt Mattie slapped the dasher up and down so fast I thought the churn would turn over.

No point in arguing that a Rednell had not shot Uncle Cade. That was as clear as the sunshine in July. After that, though, things got muddy. I just knew, like most people, that Mr. Rednell had done it, but apparently there was not enough proof to bring him to trial. "Reasonable doubt," somebody always said. Anyway, for certain, Aunt Mattie didn't harbor any love in her heart for the Rednells and I was to leave the subject alone.

Actually a year or so later, for the general public, if not for Aunt Mattie, the mystery was cleared up.

Marvin, we heard, had gotten into trouble down in the Piedmont and hopped a train heading west, supposedly to find his brother in Washington state. Before he got across the Rockies, though, he simply disappeared into thin air. His older brother had a letter from him saying he was going to explore some old mines and also saying that he wasn't sorry he'd shot the sheriff. When, weeks later, Marvin had not shown up, the brother sent the letter to the Jackson County courthouse. The law checked the handwriting with a sample from the school and since it matched, Mr. Rednell was no longer the chief suspect. He was pretty much a full-fledged drunk by then, and people steered clear of him and his stinking breath. Plus he was a sick man, everybody said. I thought Aunt Mattie would be glad to know for sure who did it, but she just set her mouth straighter. I heard her and Mrs. Hall talking one day about the Rednells, Marvin in particular.

"That Marvin was always a mighty clever boy," Mrs. Hall said.

"Mighty likely to get into trouble," Aunt Mattie agreed.

"Guess they'll find Marvin's bones in some goldmine shaft one of these years," was Mrs. Hall's opinion.

"Not likely," Aunt Mattie said. "He could be sitting pretty out there somewhere, free as a bird and we'd never know it." She settled her elbows on the rocker's arms. "Might even be logging up in Alaska, living like a Eskimo."

"They've got WANTED posters up all over that state the letter was from," Mrs. Hall said. "So the postmaster told me."

"And a lot of good it'll do." Aunt Mattie pulled her sweater closer. "Mighty convenient, I'd say, confessing like that."

"You still think the old man done it?" Mrs. Hall said.

"Him or somebody," Aunt Mattie replied. "That's all I'm going to say."

IN THOSE YEARS, Aunt Mattie came to rely on me to keep things straight. She never remarried although she was still young enough, I guess. I asked Aunt Mattie why she didn't get married again, especially after Bran Hyatt came calling a few times. They'd sit on the porch and talk a little, but she wasn't much for talking and Bran was known to be shy. He was a widower, though, and had a good job at the tannery. He smelled slightly of turpentine, but he had a full set of his own teeth and a nice smile.

"There's not a man in this world I can't do without," Aunt Mattie said.

"Well, you'd have somebody...."I couldn't finish that sentence. Nobody talked about bedrooms, at least not grownups.

"I'm finished with all that foolishness," Aunt Mattie said. She turned back to rolling dough for fried apple pies. Then she concentrated on placing the apples in the center of each square of dough.

"We get along all right without men, don't we, June?"

"Yep," I said. And it was true. Men came to plow her garden, but we planted it, hoed it, weeded it, harvested it, and canned it. Men came to clean the well or to repair the roof, to shore up the edge of the porch. And once in a while, one wanted to sit longer on the porch than was necessary to drink buttermilk or coffee. Only Bran persisted, and then he gave up and married a girl from Macon County who was awfully young for him.

Aunt Mattie got a small pension of some kind, her "government check," but as I grew and needed clothes and wanted books, and as the house needed repairs, she went to work on a public job. She cooked at the big hotel in Dillsboro, rising early to get her famous biscuits in the oven and staying until mid-afternoon. Since she had let Uncle Cade's car go back "for the payments," the manager picked her up or sent someone for her. Occasionally if she worked in the evenings, I went with her. I'd sit behind the reception desk, staying out of the way.

I spent some of my time reading, most of it watching. Truthfully, while I held a book in my hands, I listened, paying attention to the comings and goings in the hotel. The hotel guests were a people a world apart. I didn't know what to make of them. They seemed like books to me, every one a story. And from the snippets of conversations, I invented pasts and presents for them. They didn't talk like most people I knew, and I found out they felt the same about me and the hotel workers. I learned we were "locals." One woman asked me a question one day involving more than a "Yes, ma'am" or "No ma'am." When I answered, she called to her companion, "Anthony, listen to this little mountain girl. Doesn't she sound just precious, so quaint."

"Sounds like all the rest of these locals, I suppose," Anthony said. "Leave the kid alone."

The funny part was that she sounded strange to me, I mean even stranger than the other guests. After they left, I asked the manager where they were from.

"Lordy, they're from way up north. New York City, she said. The Bronx, he said."

"Is that the same place?"

"Don't ask me."

153

Aunt Mattie Goes to the Dentist

"I'D RATHER BE a knot on a hickory tree than to have to go to the dentist," Aunt Mattie said. She adjusted her black hat and made a face at her image in the mirror. Her left jaw was so swollen that she couldn't really pull much of a frown, and when she let her guard down I could see the pain in her eyes.

"Can't I go with you?" I'd never been inside a dentist's office. Everybody said I was blessed with good strong teeth, but I was curious about what the kids at school called the torture chamber.

"No. I told you Addie and her brother's coming by to get me. She's getting a permanent wave while I'm at the dentist's."

I thought I'd like to see a permanent wave being given plus see the teeth-puller's torture room. Aunt Mattie thought I shouldn't waste my time.

"You've got schoolwork to do, young lady. And the other chores you've been laying off to get done."

It was true I had been so busy reading *Lorna Doone* lately that I had neglected a few things around the house. Aunt Mattie didn't expect me to do a whole lot, but I'd promised to split kindling and to re-stack the woodpile that had fallen down two weeks before.

"I'll have supper ready," I promised. If Aunt Mattie could have smiled without hurting, she would have. I saw the little gleam in her eyes. Cooking was not something that came naturally to me.

"Just some soup beans, June. I won't be able to chew anything anyway."

It was dark when Addie and her brother brought Aunt Mattie home. Luckily I had fixed a big pot of beans and the cornbread was in the warming oven. When all three came in the front door, I knew we'd have company for supper.

Brad Schuler put his hat on the peg and settled himself in front of the fireplace. The women looked exhausted. They came in the kitchen.

"Run get some kraut, June, and I'll fry us some potatoes."

"Are you all right?" The swelling had gone down some in Aunt Mattie's jaw, but her lips were drawn to the left. I had some trouble understanding her instructions.

"Yes. Minus not one but two teeth." She was already picking potatoes out of the bin and fumbling for a paring knife.

"Sit down, Aunt Mattie," I said. "You look done in. I'll get the potatoes started in just a minute. Everything else is ready."

It surprised me that my aunt left off what she was doing and joined Addie at the kitchen table. As I hurried past her, I saw in the semi-darkness Addie's hair.

"What in the world?" I dashed out before I finished, knowing what I was about to say was uncomplimentary. Addie's gray hair was frizzled up in little tight kinks that made her head look like nothing I'd ever seen.

In record time, we were seated at the table and I poured buttermilk for all of us. I was proud of my first "cooking for company" supper, even if it was just ordinary fare, no chicken or ham. Brad Schuler set right in to eating. He looked up only once to say, "Good potatoes, June. You'll make some man a good cook one of these days."

After that one comment, like he'd uncorked a bottle, both women started talking.

"Lord, Mattie, don't talk to me about the tooth-puller!" Addie crumbled bread into her beans. "If you want your head fried, and your brains just about jolted out of your head, go to Thelma's. If I'd a-knowed what I was in for—"

"Well, I'd risk that any day, compared to that dentist chair." Aunt Mattie's voice quivered just a little. I couldn't believe it. I'd seen her deal with burns and cuts and stonebruises and bad headaches without more than a word or two of complaint.

"What happened?" I asked.

Both women answered at the same time.

"He set me down in this cold as cream chair, I was surrounded by these little instruments, picks and tweezers, and before I knew—"

"Thelma's got this contraption with wires coming down in all directions—Addie chimed in.

"This ain't going to hurt much, Miz Geer' is what he said. 'But I've got to look in there. Open up.'"

"And Thelma took these chemicals out of this bottle and that bottle, smelling to high heaven—"

"I'd put my glasses on this little tray beside the chair, so I couldn't see right clearly, but I saw that needle in his hand. 'Lord, Doc,' I said, 'is that meant for me?' I could see that needle sharp enough and that dentist's teeth. Now he's got the prettiest teeth I've ever seen on a man. True pearly whites. I started to tell him just give me a pill or two—"

"Thelma's got a washing chair, and she had my neck bent backwards and my head in that wash basin before I could say more'n that I wanted a permanent wave, fine as she give Miz Duffey last month. Long as I can remember this was the first time anybody's fingers have been scrubbing my head besides mine. The shampoo just foamed up. She's got a way with washing hair, I'll tell you. My head won't recover till a month of Sundays."

"'Bad luck, Miz Geer, there are two molars that will have to come out, truth be told, I ought to delay on one of them, a little abscess there. You do want them out, don't you? This will sting a little.' How was I supposed to answer, me with my head in these little padded cushions and a big white cloth clipped to me. He kept on talking, mumbling this and that and waving that needle around. I had both eyes wide open, but I couldn't say a thing. Now, that needle part was the scariest part, when it scrunched right on into my gums, I thought I'd die."

"And the minute Thelma pushed me back straight up after a-rinsing and a-rinsing, she started in with them wires, just a-twisting this way and that. Then she started attaching me to that machine, clamping me tight as a drum. Lordy, all I could think about was that electric chair in Raleigh."

"Funny thing, after I thought I'd die, I kind of lost track of what was going on. Then all of a sudden, I thought my face was going to come apart from my head! I could hear this scrunching and wrenching and pulling and tearing, and I had to hold on to the chair or I believe he'd have pulled us both right out of that chair and through the wall and down Main Street, it was that bad. There was a sucking sound—"

"My hair was all twisted up and Thelma was a-humming to herself, halfway talking, things like 'your hair's coarse, it'll take a wave just fine, am I hurting you' and all the time my eyeballs are being pulled back to China, they'll never be the same—"

It was all I could do to keep looking back and forth from one to the other.

"This sucking sound, and he said 'Ah, that's the worst one. Might as well go ahead while you're here. You feel anything?' What could I say, blood gushing out as it was and me with my head over that little sink. I was spitting like crazy and feeling this big hole in my mouth, and—"

"Well, she turned on the power and I swear I heard my head a-sizzlin. I smelled something burning too and I said—"

"You know I couldn't say a word, my lips wouldn't work right. Now that's a funny feeling. You got something to say, though I don't know if I would have said stop or get the other one, and not a word come out. In a flash he was back in my mouth and I held on to the chair while he pulled and twisted. I was sweating by then. What a blessed relief when he held up the tooth, and I started spitting blood again. Now I hope that's the last time I ever darken the door of that or any other dentist."

I shivered and put my hand on Aunt Mattie's arm.

"'Thelma,' I hollered, 'you're a-burning my head up!' I was getting pigsick of that smell and all them potions she used before hand. If I'd been out of doors I'd have puked right there."

Addie covered her mouth with her hand. She realized she'd said a word that wasn't for the supper table.

"I mean it, Mattie. Still Thelma just come over and untwisted one of the curls and said I'd need a few more minutes."

"That smell's enough to turn a man's stomach," her brother said. "Good thing your man's working in Yancey County."

"You shut your mouth, Brad Schuler. Don't talk like that in front of June."

"Do you hurt now, Aunt Mattie?"

"I'm feeling better, just got what feels like two of them—what did you tell me about last week, June? Two big craters in my jaw. I'll be fine. But never again will I darken his door."

"And Thelma, she charged me extra for some fine spray she used. That's likely what you're talking about, brother. You don't know a fancy smell when you smell one."

Aunt Mattie must have gotten her lips under control. She smiled at me and said to her friend, "Of the two of us, Addie, it's a toss-up as to who got the worst deal. But my ordeal don't show!"

Sitting With Annie

AFTER UNCLE CADE'S funeral, I didn't see PeeDee for almost three years. No one replaced her in my heart. The girls at school made tentative friendship moves, but I couldn't make my heart respond. I moved like a sprite for months, like a feather caught in air currents, weightless, drifting, settling nowhere solid. Yet, in every way that showed, my life was as solid as a gold dollar and just as remote to me. I went to school and made good grades. Good grades were so easy for me that they didn't really matter.

I wrote to PeeDee every week for a year or so, telling her what was happening. But not much was happening without her to share it with. She was right. She wasn't much for writing, and her two short letters were awkward and lifeless, not like the PeeDee I cherished as my special friend. PeeDee went to a big brick school and didn't like it or dislike it. She said she was "indifurent" to it. One sentence in her second letter bothered

me: "Don't go mourning over me, June. I ain't worth it."
PeeDee had always had a sense of her worth, so I didn't know
what to make of that. I was glad she signed the letter "Love,
PeeDee."

PeeDee came back to Jackson County a few times. One
time they visited Mr. Rednell in the hospital when everybody
thought he was dying. Another time Aunt Mattie said PeeDee
came to see me while the rest of her family went to the jail to
visit her father. He was occasionally thrown in jail for one thing
or another: indecent exposure, attempted rape, assault. That
time I was at a 4-H weekend camp, learning to do things I'd
seen done all my life and did not want to do when I grew up:
crochet, knit, quilt, and cook. Aunt Mattie said it'd do me good
to get out with other girls, and the Snyder sisters asked me to go
with them in their new Buick. Louellen and Louanne and I got
along fine, but when we talked we were careful with our words.

Another time I missed seeing PeeDee because Aunt Mattie
and I went to Bruton's Mountain. With Grandma and Grandpa
and Johnnie gone, and the Watsons owning their land, the
whole place was like another world. People said that old Lash
roamed the mountain, acting more and more like a wolf,
growling at anybody who didn't belong there.

But that day, even though I didn't get to see PeeDee, I was
glad to be where I was. Annie gave me a gift that "passeth
understanding" as the preachers would say. And it was only a
few words that one time I went to Bruton's mountain after what
I came to call my abandonment. That's the word Annie used,
and it had such a long drawn out bunch of sounds with that
"done" in the middle. We sat on her porch. I was surprised
when she brought out a beer for herself and handed me a glass
of cold milk.

"Since we got electricity now, I'm getting addicted to these
things," she said, flourishing the brown bottle. "I know your
mama'd rather see me with one of these than dipping snuff. She
couldn't stand that." She drank with satisfaction. "I've give that
habit up."

Nobody had spoken to me so naturally about mama in a long time, used the word so easily. People just didn't bring up the subject around me.

"Mama..." I said.

Annie now looked uncomfortable.

"They just left me behind," I said. I wasn't going to cry, not now. I'd gotten over that.

"To a better life, June," she said. "That's why your daddy abandoned you. He couldn't—he thought he couldn't take care of you and Rose, not on what he could make around here, not with what she needed." She looked at the angry bees on the morning glory vines.

"Your ride will be here any minute and I've been wondering what to tell you, if anything. God knows, Mattie never will and somebody should talk to you, but sometimes," she said, "knowledge hurts."

"Sometimes it's a good thing," I said. "Sometimes I think I don't know nothing."

Annie grinned. The beer had put some life into her eyes. "You know better than that!" She was talking about my grammar. She'd always paid strict attention to my grammar.

"Please tell me, Annie."

"Not much to tell. Your mama just slid deeper and deeper into some pit of her own making. Pitch black unhappy. She was getting dangerous close to doing harm, to you, to Carl, more likely herself. Some women, June, aren't made for mothering. Me, I reckon I am. Don't know why me and Rose got along as good as we did. Rose didn't want kids and she didn't pay enough attention to, to not having them, well, to not get herself...pregnant."

Annie had hesitated as if I'd never heard the word.

"She had a couple of miscarriages, you know that, I guess. Anyway, miscarriage is what we pretended they was. She was desperate not to have another baby, and Carl, well, Carl loved you so much."

Annie's eyes filled with tears.

160

"Mercy, I should never have started on this," she said. She looked at me. I picked at some specks on my new shirt.

"Carl, well, he was always kind of weak when it come to your mama. Loved her too much maybe. I'm not telling this too well. Anyway, after they heard about William and then after his folks...was gone, he saw signs. We all did that your mama was getting more and more unstable."

Annie sat silently for long moments. "One time she said she'll kill you if it meant getting away from here. These mountains closed her in. When she said it again, Carl talked to Cade and Mattie. They'd noticed the way Rose was acting. They said they'd like a girl around."

Annie finished her beer and tossed the bottle onto a pile of trash to the side of the yard.

"I heard that Cade said they'd be glad to keep you, but it wouldn't be good to keep interrupting your life, coming and going. If they was gonna go, you'd need to grow up without being pulled in ever which way. I don't know this for sure, but my impression is that Cade thought it would be better for you not to hear from them at all."

My glass of milk on the floor by my chair had two bees in it, flapping or trying to swim. I watched them trying to get out of that milk and back into the air. I realized Annie was watching me, waiting for me to say something.

"Might not have been the best advice Cade ever handed out. Rose was always a kind of nuisance to him. He thought she should've stayed in Georgia. Reckon he just didn't know...and if he said to leave you for good, Carl may be trying to honor that, so's you have..."

Finally I picked up the milk and splashed it over the edge of the porch into the morning glories. I couldn't see if the bees found their way out of the vines.

"Here comes your ride now. Ain't it good the Watsons got this road fixed so a truck can get up here? You get to set in the back, looks like." She waved to the driver. "Mattie's got one of them little Watson girls on her lap, taking her to Sylva to stay with a cousin and get some doctoring."

"Annie, please," I didn't exactly know what I wanted to know that could be told in a minute.

"Your daddy's up in Norfolk now, Robert said. Somebody in the Piedmont said he'd seen him up there, talked to him a minute. Working in the shipyards, I think he said."

I stood up. Aunt Mattie yelled, "We can't stop to visit, Annie. We have to get this little one to the doctor. Come on, June."

"And, June, your mama, Rose," Annie cleared her throat. "Lord, I liked her in spite of her ways. Rose is getting some help. It takes every penny Carl makes right now to pay her bills."

I was at the porch's edge, looking at Aunt Mattie holding a child. "I bet I won't ever see them again."

"Oh, honey, I think you will." She sighed. "Your daddy anyway. Your daddy'll come back. This is his home. He's just lost right now."

"Abandonment," I said.

"Sometimes, a man don't have a lot of choices," Annie said. "Try to remember that."

In a surprise move, she stood up and gave me a quick hug, the same kind of hug she'd given me when Grandma died. I wasn't used to hugs. I wrapped my arms around her thickening waist. I wanted to thank her. But the words wouldn't come. I said, "Bye, Annie."

I scrambled into the back of the truck and waved to her. She looked so lonesome sitting there without a beer and all her children somewhere else.

Going Dowsing

"SARAH'S GETTING A dowser to find water on her place," Aunt Mattie said. We were sitting on the front porch at dusk. She thumbed through a new Sears Roebuck catalog.

When I wasn't watching lightening bugs, I was doing my arithmetic homework, figuring out word problems where people wanted to determine the strangest things for no good reason. In class while Miss Johnson was explaining how to slice a cake mathematically when seven people showed up for dinner, Willie spoke up. "My mama can slice a cake into eleven even slices without doing all this figuring—and still give the preacher a bigger piece."

"Yeah, and who's ever going to try to figure how much faster a train's gonna..." and one or two other pupils, emboldened by the daring of Willie, joined in.

The teacher almost had a commotion on her hands, but she quelled it in a hurry. "These problems are to make you think, Will, and it's not your mama who'll be tested on them on Friday." We settled back down to thinking, figuring, erasing, and thinking some more.

Now I was figuring on a train going fifty miles an hour for the first forty-five minutes and then slowing down and the engineer wondering about how many miles they'd have to travel at ten miles more per hour in order to be only fifteen minutes late at the station eighty miles away. At Aunt Mattie's words, I perked up.

"A water witching?"

I'd heard about dowsing and knew the names of the two or three people who had reputations for finding water. But I'd never actually seen anybody dowse. Aunt Mattie nodded.

"Can I go watch?"

"We'll see. I might walk over to Sarah's myself. It's been a while since I've seen her."

"Don't you want to see the dowsing?" I couldn't imagine that visiting with Sarah, whose children were all grown and gone except Barbie, could equal actually finding water in the company of a dowser.

"Don't know that I rightly believe in that anyway," Aunt Mattie said. "But Sarah's desperate to get a good water supply.

They've been carrying water from across at Hyatts for a month by now. Guess she'll try anything, even Avery."

Johnson Avery was already at Sarah's when we arrived. He was tall and thin, and his long sleeved shirt cuffs left his bony wrists bare. He carried his dowsing rod, a forked stick about three feet long, and for such an important instrument, I thought he handled it rather casually. I looked closely at the stick. It looked ordinary enough to me, a willow stick, not like something that could divine the presence of underground water.

A cigarette extended from the dowser's mouth and all the time he talked, it never fell out. He peered into the long-since dry well in the back yard, surveyed the cleared land, the cornfield, the browned garden, the nine acres or so of pastureland that was all that Sarah had left of her family farm. She'd sold off a few acres at a time to pay emergency bills like when her youngest boy had to have his tonsils out. If she didn't have a good water supply, she'd never sell the land even if she wanted to.

"June's bound and determined to see a water witching," Aunt Mattie told Sarah. She spoke as if she didn't want to directly ask Avery, and, of course, he heard.

"Won't hurt if she tags along, will it?" Sarah cleared it with the dowser.

"Long as she don't interfere," he drawled. "Stays out of my way."

"Don't you go out of sight of this house, you hear," Aunt Mattie said. I looked around. Unless the cornfield with its stand of uncut and drying fodder concealed me, I'd be pretty much in plain sight all the time.

"And watch out for snakes. They ain't gone in yet." Sarah added the usual admonition. I wondered if ever, during snake season, anybody under sixteen ever wandered beyond the yard or garden without hearing those words. Barefoot or in shoes, we stayed "on alert" all the time.

Johnson Avery walked slowly, starting at the edge of the yard, for several yards straight ahead. He held the forked stick directly in front of him, his eyes focused on the air beyond the stick. I trailed behind and slightly to the left so I could see what was happening. For a long time nothing was.

He stopped, walked to the right a few steps, then back toward the house. I figured out he was covering all the land in a kind of sweeping, arcing pacing. It was slow and tedious work. Once in a while, he stopped, stuck the dowsing rod in the hook on his overalls, lit up a cigarette, and took a few puffs before beginning again. Dowsing was smoking work for him, thirsty work for me.

For almost two hours I trailed along. I watched intently every time Avery hesitated or stopped entirely, but I never said a word. I couldn't tell if the dowsing stick was telling him anything. He seemed almost in a trance, the forked stick an extension of his long arms. When he stopped for a cigarette, he simply looked up at the sky, now a hazy pale blue, or at the lay of the land. In my mind he was taking on the qualities of a magician, like that Merlin way back in the time of King Arthur, a sorcerer able to see into the secrets of the earth. After a cigarette break, though, he became human again.

"Stay here," he commanded. As if I would move anywhere except to follow him. He walked a few yards away, into the edge of the cornfield, and turned his back. I knew what he was doing, and it made me want to pee, too. But I didn't want to miss anything, and I was not going to ask him to wait while I found a hidden spot. I would endure the pressure. I just squatted down and waited for him, stirring in the dust and watching a ladybug.

"Water's under here somewheres," he said. He must have tired of the dusty silence and was ready to talk to any ears nearby. I moved a step closer.

"Reckon water lines is just like veins in a person's body, some's more hidden than others, but the liquid's gonna flow." He paced carefully, as if he'd not be outdone by the concealed veins beneath our feet.

I ventured a comment. "Like some people's fat and you can't see their veins?"

"This don't look like fat land," he said, the cigarette bobbing slightly, "but yeah, something like that. Sometimes, them waterlines is too far down to make it worth the effort to get to the surface. Might be the case here, but I wouldn't of thought so."

I pondered on his words. It looked like that dowsing stick was never going to show us anything. I remembered Aunt Mattie's words at Mrs. Rednell's baptizing.

I said, "Do you think some people's like that too, and keep their feelings way deep?"

It must have been the sun, my sense of isolation from the women back at the house, my feeling that we were two alone, adventurers cut off from the security of walls and routine, or I wouldn't have thought of asking Mr. Avery something like that. I halfway hoped he hadn't heard or wouldn't answer.

"It's a fact of human nature, same as water or sky nature," he said. "There's them with feelings at their skin tips. Slightest prick'll send them off and they'll tell you anything. Then there's deep 'uns." Mr. Avery walked even more slowly, as if waiting for something.

"Most people'll got something buried inside them they'd not willingly show, I reckon," he said. "Most got good reasons for it."

I imagined all the earth and all the water on its surface, visible. On the maps always blue or greenish blue, in the river and pond sometimes brown, sometimes clear. And all the water underneath us, deep, shallow, racing, whirlpooling. The ground grew uneasy under my feet, like I was stepping in thick mud. My head swirled.

"Hey, watch out!" Mr. Avery caught me as I slipped downward. In an instant he steadied me and I looked up and focused on the cigarette at his lips. I shook my head to clear it. I was embarrassed and stammered, "I,I kind of blacked out and my feet—they didn't—I thought the ground moved."

"You okay to stand now, young'un? Here, set down a minute. Should have brought a jar of water with us." He looked closely at me, a question in his face.

"Maybe too much sun," he muttered. Then, as I sat down, avoiding a thistle, he said, "Or maybe something else."

He picked up his dowsing rod from the dirt, dusted it off with a wipe of his hand, and crouched over closer to the ground. I wish I'd watched every move, but I put my head down for a few moments, trying to reconstruct the feeling that had made me think I was sinking. When I looked up, Mr. Avery was several yards away, intent and purposeful. He held the rod straight in front of him and would shift first one way, then drift in a slightly different angle.

Tall and loose-jointed as he was, he reminded me of a ship, of what I imagined a sailboat would be like, sort of skimming along, not in a fast wind but not weighted down low in the water, like a picture we'd seen of an Egyptian boat. I stood up, careful not to make any noise, and eased through the field until I was about three feet behind and to the side, so I could see what was happening.

This was it, I thought. He'd found water and I hadn't even been watching at the crucial time. He paid no attention to me. I couldn't tell that the dowsing stick was doing anything, but Mr. Avery was giving it his full attention and a little smile played about his lips. In fact, the cigarette was burning steadily away very close to his lips. Without breaking his smooth gliding stride, he simply opened his mouth and let the lighted stub fall to the ground. I raked some loose dirt over it and stepped on the mound.

On up the hill we went, and then Mr. Avery stopped, studied the ground, studied the dowsing rod, waited. He made a half circle to the left, then back to where he'd stopped, then to the right, and back almost to the original spot.

"Right about here," he said. He stuck the stick in the ground, and took another cigarette from the packet. I surveyed the ground. It looked no different, no richer, no damper, no greener than any other spot. It was some yards down from a clump of evergreens.

"How'd you know, for sure?" I hoped my question didn't insult him.

"There's a water vein runs down this way," he said. "If it don't start right here, it's close about. I'll stake my gold watch on it."

I didn't see any gold watch on his wrists, but maybe he left it at home when he put his faith in the dowsing rod.

"Bring me two or three big rocks from around here to mark the spot," he directed. I piled up several rocks at the water spot while he smoked, his hands in his pockets, his eyes fixed on the line of trees at the end of the pasture.

"Get you a well dug up there where the young'un here piled some rocks," he told Sarah, pointing toward the evergreens. "Chances are for a good supply, I'd say. I was about to give up hope," he went on, "till this young'un like to have passed out. Standing on a power line she was, is my guess. I'd missed it."

Aunt Mattie and Sarah looked at me and I was puzzled. Had I helped the water witching? I don't know. Johnson Avery drove away in his old truck without elaborating.

Aunt Mattie remained unconvinced. "Sarah and me had a good visit," she said as we walked home. "But I wouldn't put my faith in Johnson Avery's water witching. I don't trust that man. He's got secret eyes."

We walked on. Me, I would have bet my last nickel on the water being there, but I couldn't exactly say why to Aunt Mattie. "Besides," she said, "he's not from around here and I heard he's been in jail over in Yancey County." For a fact, Aunt Mattie didn't trust anybody the law had ever seen fit to lock up.

But two weeks later, Sarah had a new well with more water than anybody would have thought possible even if it was a good piece from her house. I pondered on the dowsing. Not so much the way I felt when my feet seemed to give way, but the way Mr. Avery moved along through the field afterwards, like the ground was his ocean and he had a breeze to his back. That vision stayed with me and I didn't want to share it with anybody, not even Aunt Mattie.

The Truth Came By Train

NOBODY ELSE—EXCEPT PeeDee—knows that I know who killed Uncle Cade. Several people know who did the deed, and some of them may in time, for love or other reasons, tell others, but only PeeDee knows that I know.

PeeDee's mama and her brothers and sisters know, but none of them will likely be telling. Her brother Marvin, wherever he is, won't ever surface under his own name again. He took it upon himself to lay claim to the crime—to protect the killer. They all had the family to think of.

It's a secret that I have to deal with, a sacred trust. When I realized that love means leaving and staying, and love means keeping secrets, I grew up. With that burden of knowledge and bond of silence, I reckoned I could deal with anything the world set before me.

The train didn't stop at Dillsboro unless there was some good reason. But it slowed down and on Tuesday, in late October. I waited just beyond the trestle. PeeDee had sent me a letter. "I'm coming through on the afternoon train. Some Tuesday in October, don't know which one. Meet me at the dip. I can't stay long, just till the next train."

The letter came on the twenty-eighth of September. For three Tuesdays I scrambled through the woods and waited for the whistle of the train. Three Tuesdays it had slowed down before chugging on through town. One time, my heart pounded as a figure swung, as if from long practice, from the half-opened door of a boxcar. It was a bearded man, though, and I stayed behind the dusty clump of bushes. I wondered what he was doing in our parts: returning to a dear mother, bringing news of a loved one to a family, rescuing some unloved girl from her boyfriend. Maybe he just liked riding trains and stopping off in different places. Not knowing anybody, not connecting to anything. I could understand that.

I knew in my bones, as the whistle sounded this time, that PeeDee would be on the train. I hoped she'd practiced jumping off trains down in the Piedmont. The bearded man had made it seem easy enough, but it looked dangerous to me.

As the engine steamed by, I held my breath, starting counting boxcars. Toward the end, a boxcar door was open and I saw a bundled-up figure with a scarf around the neck and face, but surely it was PeeDee. The train was traveling awfully fast, too fast, and I ran out of my hiding place. The bundled figure leaned out and sort of rolled in a doubled-up way onto the ground.

For a moment, between the rushing train and my racing feet, a great void in time and motion occurred. Like when I licked my tongue to a banana popsicle and it stuck there, that awful moment between knowing and doing something about it. Frozen like time never is. Just as I reached the figure, PeeDee's hand unwrapped the scarf and I heard a yelp.

"PeeDee," I knelt beside her. "Are you okay? Did you break anything?" The yelp didn't sound like a person in pain or even like a person.

She unrolled her body and slowly sat up. "The breath's knocked out of me," she muttered. Her eyes were shining with her success—and seeing me, but she put her head down for a moment and breathed carefully.

"Look what I brought you," she said. She had on two heavy coats and under them a little face poked out. A dog. She had not only come to see me, she'd brought a dog.

"Boy, I'm warm," she said. She stood up and we hugged awkwardly, with the dog between us. "I wore all these clothes to break the fall." She grinned. "And they done the trick. Both of us made it, looks like."

The little head wiggled further out. It was brown with some black around the alert eyes, ears standing up.

"What kind is it? Where'd you get it?"

"Its name is Butch," PeeDee said. "And it's a girl. The soldiers called it Butch."

"Soldiers?"

"This here dog's been trained down at Fort Bragg." She drew the dog out completely and handed her to me. I cuddled the animal to me. She fit right into my arms.

"Better set her down for a minute to do her business," PeeDee advised. "She's been shut up in these coats for a few hours."

I instantly put Butch on the ground and she proved PeeDee right. She nosed around just a little and came right back to us, looking at PeeDee. Her tail wagged.

"Nope. Go to your new owner," PeeDee said. I stooped and picked Butch up. She licked my face.

"I never had a dog—not in my whole life."

"Yeah. Well, this one's yours. Forever." PeeDee shed her coats and we started walking away from the tracks. A few yards away, out of sight of the train tracks, we spread the coats on the ground. The sun was going down, but it was still warm. PeeDee looked thoughtful. "I reckon your Aunt Mattie'll let you keep her?"

"I'm keeping her," I said. "No matter what." Aunt Mattie didn't like dogs especially, and certainly not in the house. After Uncle Cade's death, she gave his fox hunting dogs to Deputy Jones. "Dogs are nothing but trouble," was her philosophy. But I'd convince her. This little dog was not going to sleep outside. She would stay right next to me.

"A soldier boy gave her to me," PeeDee said. "She was being trained to be a spy dog, but she don't like the sound of guns. Thunder, neither. She hightails it under the bed at the sound of thunder, even before the sound. She can hear it before we do, or maybe she smells it." PeeDee put her head on her knees. "So they were going to do away with her. Look how little she is, but she's full-grown. She's German shepherd, I think. But she's been bred to be small."

171

Butch settled into my lap, warm and comfortable, but she pointed her face toward PeeDee and watched her every move. I stroked her head. "She does look for all the world like the Watsons' big shepherds," I said. "You sure she won't get real big?"

"Sure as he—heck," PeeDee said. "The soldier boy says she's smart as a whip, but no good for what they wanted her for." There was a trace of bitterness in her voice. "So they was going to destroy her. He saved her and give her to me."

I was curious about the soldier boy and about PeeDee's life and her family. She'd tell me or not, that much I knew about PeeDee. She was taller and her freckles had disappeared. So had her pigtails.

The little dog quivered under my touch and turned her head to lick my hand. PeeDee watched. We didn't say anything, just sat quiet for a moment or two.

"Aunt Mattie's doing all right," I said, finally. "I went to 4-H Camp this summer."

PeeDee nodded.

"Everybody okay in your family?" Sitting so close, she suddenly seemed a million miles away.

"Yeah. Mama's working at the cotton mill, doing okay. The kids are in school, but Benjy's gonna drop out, I can tell. Marvin you know about."

She shifted and reached into a pants pocket. "Me, I survive." She pulled out a packet and some matches. "I smoke now." She put a Lucky Strike in her mouth and scratched a match on a rock beside her.

"Guess you're all grown up," I said. Tears were sneaking up from my stomach, but I squelched them. I petted Butch and brushed a fly away.

"I don't go to school much," PeeDee said. "Shucks, I'm smarter than most of them girls." She shrugged. "There's so many families with kids around there the schools can't keep up with us most of the time."

"Don't you have a regular house, an address where they could find you?"

"Oh, yeah. We got a little white house, even got a bathroom in it. But the school officials don't pay much attention to the likes of us. Sometimes I make a little money cleaning houses for people. They think I'm sixteen already."

"You do look older," I said.

"Older and wiser, June. That's me. The way I figure it, I can't just hang around Gastonia all my life. I'm not working in no cotton mill. I'm going on from here."

"Going where? Now? You can stay with us!"

"No, I can't. You know I can't. Your Aunt Mattie—and it's not just her. With Daddy still on the prowl around here, no, I'm just staying till the night train. It practically stops up at Balsam. I can hop on it easy."

"But, but, you're not nearly sixteen yet. What can you do? Where will you go?"

"If I'm lucky, I'll end up out in the state of Washington somewhere. You know I've got a brother out there." She lay back on the ground so I couldn't see her eyes. Her hands looked different. She'd painted her fingernails, and they were long. She'd always bitten them to the quick. Now they were rounded and glossy red.

"Marvin's alive." She spoke softly. "We had to pretend he's dead, but he's out there somewhere. Buddy won't say it, but we can read between the lines. I'll find him, I reckon."

She turned toward me. "I've thought and thought about it, June. I've got to go. You've got to stay."

How could she have known that I was about to propose that I go with her, me and Butch, too? It was on the tip of my tongue, and then she said that. My mouth was already open to tell her I'd, me and Butch'd go anywhere. I didn't want to lose her again.

"You've got to stay," she repeated, almost roughly. "I know you'd go in a New York minute. But I travel best alone."

"But—but—"

"You'd slow me down, June. You know you would. You think too much. You study on things. Me, I'll just go the way the wind blows."

Butch yelped and twisted on my lap. I hadn't realized I was squeezing him so hard.

"I'm afraid for you," I said.

"Don't worry about me. The soldier boy, his name is Wayne, his family's out in Nebraska. He told me to stop there. I may stay there awhile. I may have a baby there." She held up her hand before I could say anything. "I don't know for sure yet. But Wayne told me their address and he said he'd write them and tell them a mountain girl may show up on their doorstep. Don't know how long it'll take me. I'm in no hurry, just as long as it's before real cold weather."

"Wayne must be special," I choked.

"He's a soldier boy, first and foremost. Nineteen years old. Got red hair. I'm the only girl he's ever got in trouble, if he has. He's good to me."

PeeDee sat up and circled her knees with her arms. "He's never hit me, not once." She touched Butch's nose. "I told him I was giving Butch to you. You're my best friend in this world."

My tears dripped onto Butch's back and rolled off her sleek fur. She lay very still.

"Listen," PeeDee said, ignoring my tears. But her voice was scratchy. "It's a long walk up to Balsam. I can make it if I start now, and maybe I'll get on tonight's train. You got to get on home. Your aunt'll worry about you."

That was true. Aunt Mattie didn't keep an extra keen eye on me, but she always knew where I was. She trusted me. She thought I'd gone to the library.

We stood up. "You don't have even a bag with you," I said.

"Got lots of layers of clothes on and got some money in a bag tied around my neck. Got a pack of crackers and a candy bar here." She took out a squashed Mars Bar.

"I'll go get you some food and meet you at the Locust Field cemetery," I said. "I'll take Butch home and put her in the shed. That way I can walk with you part way."

When PeeDee nodded, I knew she was hungry. She punched my shoulder. "Hey, meet me at the old part of the graveyard, outside the fence." She bent and kissed Butch's wet nose. "Bye, dog."

The graveyard was generally well-kept but one section was purely a mess. Enclosed by a falling down fence, it was all overgrown. Some colored folks were buried there, and some people who'd killed themselves. Nobody would be around that section. After that, we could walk without being seen by dodging the main road and a few houses. I stopped and turned around.

"No, June. You can't go with me. You heard me." She made her voice sound just like a grown up's. That same "don't argue with me" tone.

I put Butch in the tool shed with a jar lid of water. Aunt Mattie was in the bedroom, lying down. I yelled to her. "I'm fixing me something to eat and going down to Sue's if that's all right."

"I'll be setting up at the Alisons," Aunt Mattie said. "You be back before dark." Mr. Alison had died the day before. Aunt Mattie wouldn't be home until late.

"Okay," I said. I slathered jelly into some biscuits, put three pieces of fried chicken in a bag, threw in the other biscuits. I poured some milk in a quart jar. I ran into my room and dug behind the pillow. My little pouch was there. Almost four dollars. I put it in my pocket. And I grabbed one more thing.

"Bye, Aunt Mattie." I stopped to crumble a piece of sausage from breakfast in front of Butch and to give her a quick hug. "Be quiet now," I said.

I was glad Aunt Mattie hadn't seen my tear-streaked face, and I thanked the stars that Deacon Alison, who'd lingered for months, had died in time for Aunt Mattie to be out of the house late this night.

As PeeDee and I walked from the cemetery in the general direction of Balsam, we didn't talk much. I told her little bits of gossip and about going to the bigger school in Sylva, and she told me what living in a city was like. I figured I wouldn't like it even if she did try to make it sound exciting to be able to get ice cream in cones and go to movies on Saturday, stuff like that. Finally, I told her what Annie had said: why Daddy left me, how Mama was, where they were.

I said, "I don't know if they'll ever come back." PeeDee somehow didn't seem surprised.

"Sounds like he was thinking of your own good, like daddies ought to. I betcha he comes back."

I pretended not to notice that she hadn't included Mama. So we talked and talked, but something wasn't being said.

I was glad we had a full moon, but it was still rough going, staying off the roads the way we were. I was getting tired, stumbling once in a while.

"June, this is far enough." PeeDee stopped and immediately took out her cigarettes. We sat down, squatting.

"Finish off the milk," I said. "You don't want to try to get on the train with that."

With those words, I knew I'd accepted the fact that she was going, that she was leaving. She turned the quart jar up, drank quickly, and handed it back to me. I'd take it back. Aunt Mattie would miss one of her jars. PeeDee had eaten the jelly biscuits and tucked the rest of the food into some inner pockets. "Breakfast, lunch, and dinner tomorrow," she said.

"Here, here's some money for you. It's all I've got." I handed her the bills and coins.

"I'll take it, and owe you," she said.

We were silent for a long while. I could see PeeDee twisting her hands in the darkness.

"June, I can't leave without telling you the truth."

"What truth? You're married?"

"I'm the one who shot your Uncle Cade. I killed him."

That was the farthest thing from my mind, and I let out a little gasp. Not in horror— just surprise. I watched the cigarette glow and not glow so much as she inhaled and exhaled.

"Don't hate me for it," she said. "Daddy was blind drunk and he kept coming at me all day. His intentions was plain as day. He'd done it before, but not in front of Mama and the kids. He was just blind crazy drunk."

"Coming at you? You mean he wanted to kill you?"

"No. Not kill me. Don't you know nothing?"

"Well, no, what?"

"Remember Elleree, you know, at school, the girl whose daddy—"

"Elleree King, yeah, she had a baby...oh." I could say nothing else. I wasn't even supposed to know that much. The grownups shut up if anybody mentioned Elleree and her baby. They prayed for her in church, like she was a sinner for having a baby and for keeping it.

But I'd heard some women talking on the porch when they thought I was out feeding the chickens. "That son-of-a-bitch ought to be hung by his you-know-whats," Mrs. Duffey said. That shocked me, coming from the preacher's wife. But Mrs. Hall's words shocked me even more. "That poor baby's got hisself a papa and a grandpapa all in one." They moved down to Barker's Creek not long after the baby boy was born. Elleree, her mama, her daddy, and boy Jonah.

"Well, lucky for me, I guess, I wasn't old enough to have a baby, so Daddy was safe. He'd been fooling around with me for a few months." She picked up the milk jar and threw it against a big rock. It smashed and the pieces of glass went everywhere. We covered our faces, but a tiny piece hit my hand. It bled a little.

"Mama's bound to have seen what was going on," PeeDee said. "But I didn't tell. That day Daddy was too drunk to care who knew. I kept dodging him. Marvin got after him with the axe and threatened him good, scared him some. Even that didn't slow him down for long. I got his pistol from the bedroom. I was ready to blow his brains out."

She looked around for something else to throw, but there wasn't anything. She picked up a stick and broke it with a snap. "The thing is, your uncle stepped right in the way. Right smack in the way." A choked sob shook her shoulders. "You know the rest."

The jelly biscuit I'd eaten came up and I turned aside, coughing and spitting. I wiped my mouth. I'd hate apple jelly forever. "Why didn't you tell me?" I whispered.

"I shouldn't even be telling you now," PeeDee said. "We all swore we'd keep it a secret till our dying day."

"I won't tell," I said. "I wish it'd been your daddy, though."

"Me, too." PeeDee started to bite her fingernail but clenched her hands together. "Mama's never said a word about it since, like it was my fault. I think she's glad I'm leaving. Maybe baby Lily will miss me."

"I'll miss you, PeeDee. I'll miss you forever."

I reached into my pocket. "Here, take this." I handed her the locket she'd given to me at Uncle Cade's funeral. "Except for Grandma's knife, it's all I've got of value in this world," I said. "I want you to take it with you."

PeeDee looked at the locket and then put it around her neck. "It'll go where I go," she said. She stood up and I did too. "Look, June. You've got to get back home, and I've got to get on out of here. Be good to Butch. Don't say nothing else," she said. "Except bye."

"Bye, PeeDee," I whispered. A cloud covered the moon and I didn't see her go. I heard her say, "Bye, June. Go on home, now."

"Home," I breathed as I stumbled along through the leaves and my tears. When I saw the light on at our house, I straightened up.

"I'm staying, Grandma," I said. "Aunt Mattie, I'm staying."